All Rights Reserved

REBIRTH

Emmy Ellis

Chapter One

Faith Lemon trembled. She'd wanted to do the job the man had approached her for — at the time. Now, with her son dead and the visit she'd had from his ex yesterday, she wanted nothing more than to run away. To be free of this life, one she'd long since secretly hated. She could become a new person, a *better* person, instead of the bitter and twisted cow she was. A sense of invisibility had crept in not so long ago. People didn't *see* her anymore, not properly. Age was a cruel master. She didn't have wrinkle-free skin, and her black hair came out of a bottle to hide the nasty greys. She was stuck in the middle of the menopause, experiencing every speck of the effects, and haunted by her past, what had happened, the decisions she'd made.

Remorseful, for once.

It had taken a slice to her face to get her there, though. When the blade had carved through her skin, it was as if all the stories she'd told herself to get her through life had come crashing down. She'd carefully constructed an existence that had allowed her to get up every day and face the world. Many lies, the past rewritten to suit her. Other people's decisions had moulded her into who she was today, undoubtedly, but it didn't mean she had to allow the lies to rule her. It didn't mean she could continue this life by telling herself she hadn't had a hand in how things had turned out. She could have shunned her father's teachings and been a better person a long time ago, but she hadn't, she'd preferred blaming everyone else.

She had to face up to who she was, who her parents had been, and go from there. A long road ahead, where she examined everything and owned her part in this terrible charade. She could never make up for all the hurt she'd engineered. No amount of saying sorry would cut it. So running was the best option, wasn't it? To immerse herself in a community where no one knew what she'd done, who she'd been. That idea reminded her of the time she'd wanted to run before, when she'd been *this close* to doing it, but fate had other ideas, and she'd remained where she was, here, in this house.

She'd crashed her way through so many transitions. She wasn't that innocent child anymore, brainwashed by her father. She wasn't the teen who'd— *Not that, don't think about that.* She wasn't who she'd been when she'd met Reggie, her ex-husband, nor who she'd become afterwards. Throughout his abuse she'd allowed it to happen because that was what she'd thought she deserved, that a man who raised his fists to her was right to do so. If Dad hadn't done it to Mum, she might have felt differently. For a while after Reggie had fucked off, she'd coasted along as a bitch, angry at all the wrongs she'd suffered, the world owing her, and now she'd altered yet again. The strong need to make amends had taken over, but it was useless to try. The people she'd upset didn't want to know her, and they wouldn't believe her if she turned over a new leaf anyway, saying a leopard didn't change its spots.

And how *could* she run and not do the job the man had asked her to do? The threat hanging over her—all of her neighbours knowing what she did for a living—ensured she'd obey. Having to live here until she could escape, with them throwing her nasty side-eyes because her secret had been revealed… No. Ever since Reggie had set her up as a sex worker, she'd lived in fear of her façade being discovered, worrying all the sins would come out. There were so many of them.

She worked on The Whitehall Estate in a brothel masked as a sex shop. A lot of money passed hands there, cash, and the man wanted it. She'd get a cut, something she'd need so she could set up elsewhere. If her son, nicknamed Lemon, hadn't died she'd have already done the job, would have left him behind to fix his own life, a life she'd helped create. She'd shaped him into who he'd become—a mean bastard if she were truly honest. A replica of his father. She'd morphed into her *own* father, teaching Lemon hate, stoking the fires of racism.

She shouldn't have done that. What she *should* have done was bring him up to be the opposite, but she hadn't wanted Lemon to be hurt like she had, she wanted him forewarned and forearmed. Not to have his heart shattered. Yet he'd shattered Becky's, the woman who'd given him a son. Faith had been prejudiced towards her, something that had come naturally; she'd grown up hearing *those* words and slurs. Her hatred had grown tenfold upon meeting her son's girlfriend, and she'd taken it out on Becky.

She could have reined it in. Been kind.

Except she hadn't.

Faith wouldn't be able to see her grandson, Noah, growing up. She hadn't cared about the baby until Lemon had died, when it had smacked her right in the face that she was the last one standing and she had no one else. But Becky had announced she was moving away and wouldn't say where. She had the right idea, though, getting out of London. She deserved a good life.

Faith had been awful to her. There was no excuse for her behaviour, she saw that now she'd been given a Cheshire smile that had ruined her looks. A man had come round. A ginger Scot. He'd had a go at her, told her in no uncertain terms that if she was racist again, she'd regret it.

"Change how you behave else I'll be back," he'd said and, "Get yourself educated."

She didn't know what that meant, so how would she know what to educate herself on? The twins had sent him to do their dirty work, because wasn't George's favourite punishment a Cheshire?

Serves yourself right. You shouldn't have been so bitter and close-minded. If you hadn't, your life would've been so different.

She glanced down at her phone. Read the awful message she'd received two weeks ago. She hadn't responded and was surprised the man hadn't texted her again, asking what the fuck she was playing at by ignoring him.

IT'S A GO. GET YOUR ARSE TO WORK AND DO WHAT I TOLD YOU. IF YOU DON'T…WELL, YOU KNOW HOW MUCH I LIKE STRANGLING PEOPLE, DON'T YOU…

Austin Hunt might only be thirtysomething and look like a puff of wind would knock him over, but she couldn't trust that he wouldn't use his hands on her. Her breath stalled, as if he had them around her throat right this second, squeezing.

She racked her brain for a suitable reply.

FAITH: SORRY FOR THE DELAY, BEEN GRIEVING. AND I'VE HAD MY FACE SLASHED. NEEDED STITCHES. GOT TIME OFF WORK UNTIL NEXT WEEK. EVEN THEN, I DON'T KNOW IF WHITEHALL WILL TAKE ME BACK AS I LOOK A MESS.

AH: YOU'D BETTER BE JOKING. I NEED THAT MONEY BY THE END OF THE WEEK. I TOLD YOU I ONLY HAD LIMITED TIME.

FAITH: I'M NOT MESSING AROUND! SOMEONE CAME HERE AND USED A KNIFE ON ME.

AH: YOU STUPID FUCKING COW. I TOLD YOU TO KEEP YOUR HEAD DOWN.

FAITH: I DIDN'T KNOW HE'D COME ROUND, DID I!

AH: GO TO WORK TODAY. SAY YOU'RE FEELING BETTER.

FAITH: WHAT IF SHE TELLS ME I CAN'T SERVICE THE PUNTERS?

AH: THEN ASK TO DO SOMETHING ELSE. I NEED YOU AT THAT BROTHEL. DO IT, OR I'LL BE PAYING YOU A FUCKING VISIT.

FAITH: PLEASE DON'T.

AH: I've been going to the brothel every day to look in the wheelie bin for the money, when all along you haven't even been there. What a complete dickhead.

Faith: It's not like you messaged me to find out what was going on, so don't have a go at me.

AH: Whatever.

Faith closed the message thread, tears prickling. If she had the money, she'd fuck off now and not look back. Becky had borrowed some from the twins, so could she?

Like they're going to lend you anything after they sent their man round. After what you've done…

True. They'd laugh in her ruined face. Tell her to go and fuck herself. And who could blame them? Lemon had been messing around on their turf with the Sparrow Lot, so she'd heard, and if she'd known what they'd been up to, she'd have warned Lemon to back away. To play games on The Cardigan Estate when The Brothers ran it, well, you had to be a bit thick, didn't you? Plus there were rumours Lemon was someone who'd been employed by The Network, who'd brought women over from abroad and pimped them out for sex. He'd supposedly been a killer. An assassin. She didn't believe that, though.

Did she?

He probably thought he was clever. That he'd never get caught. Like I did regarding this job, but what if Whitehall works out it's me?

Austin had assured her no one would suspect her, but how could he know that for sure? He hadn't told her the ins and outs of his plan, just that she had to nick cash from the safe, leave it out the back in the wheelie bin, and act innocent afterwards.

Four people knew the safe combination: Mrs Whitehall, Faith, Vanda, and Len the accountant. Would Whitehall think Vanda or Len had thieved? Would she get them 'sorted' when she found the money missing? The old Faith could have lived with that, but the person she was at her core, a kind and caring one who she hadn't seen hide nor hair of for decades, wouldn't be able to stand the weight of their deaths on her shoulders.

Like she couldn't stand the *other* deaths on them either. At the time, she hadn't particularly cared one jot about those people dying, but these days, the burden of guilt had plonked itself inside her and wouldn't shut up.

Becoming a new person was hard work. Facing things she didn't want to face meant seeing herself for who she'd been, and it wasn't a pretty sight.

Her mind wandered back to the job. The brothel didn't have CCTV, and Austin had known that. So he must have had help—working with one of the slappers? Which one? She hadn't seen him there as a punter, so he *had* to have inside knowledge.

Nerves pinging all over the place, she went upstairs to stare at her face. The extra smile grinned back at her, and she winced. She'd have to put makeup on even though the stitches had only been removed the other day. She was worried about infecting the nasty red scar, but she couldn't turn up like this. It wasn't gnarled, thank goodness, a clean slice, and the nurse had stitched it well, so maybe some concealer beneath foundation would work, although the cut lines across her cheeks were slightly raised. Thankfully, her gums at the back had dissolving stitches and had almost healed, so at least she could eat now instead of sipping soup through a straw.

She got to work, transforming herself, pleased with the results. If she squinted, she almost looked like she had years ago. Pretty. She was too thin to be considered curvy, but many men chose her for that, plus her age. They wanted someone more experienced. While tired of selling her body to make ends meet, she loved the ambience at the brothel. She belonged, albeit seen as part of the furniture. Whitehall had said Faith was an asset, so maybe, with the scar covered, it would be all right.

Of course, if she told her boss what Austin wanted her to do, she might be rewarded with a payment, but it wouldn't be enough to cover what she needed, and Whitehall would ask why Faith hadn't told her two weeks ago when she'd first been approached. Could she say she'd been so upset about Lemon dying that she hadn't been able to deal with it at the time? She needed a bond and a month's rent in advance. Cash to tide her over until she found another job. And what would that even be? She'd been a sex worker for so long, she wasn't sure she'd be a good fit anywhere else.

But she had to try. Living her current life had to stop.

It was time for a rebirth.

Chapter Two

*F*aith nodded at Dad as he gave one of his 'lessons'.
He was always right, everything he said came
true, so there was no way he was wrong now. He
glanced over at Mum who peeled potatoes at the sink,
her back to where he and Faith sat at the little kitchen
table.

He pointed to a picture in the newspaper. "This sort
is called a—"

"Don't!" Mum snapped. "Our Faith shouldn't be brought up like that. Don't pass on what you were taught."

Faith looked over. Mum had stiffened. Had stopped peeling. She was different lately, sticking up for herself more, chatting back to Dad. It was as if she'd turned some kind of corner, becoming a new person. She no longer flinched when Dad made any sudden moves, and she didn't let him run roughshod over her. What had happened to make her like that? Why wasn't she afraid he'd hit her now?

Dad whispered what he hadn't said, then went on with, "And this sort is a—"

"Person," Mum butted in. "They're all people. They're no different to us."

"What do you know?" Dad barked. "You haven't seen them down at the pub. Fucking think they rule the place, they do. Loads of us are sick of it."

Confused, Faith frowned. She didn't like it when Mum and Dad disagreed. Who was she supposed to believe? Dad said people who weren't white were scum, and Mum said they weren't. Faith's friend, Lucia, who lived down the road, she didn't get confused. Her parents said the same thing, that certain people ought to go back to where they'd come from. Mum said that was racial prejudice, whatever that

14

was, and she didn't like it. Dad said they didn't belong and had no right being here. Lucia said the same.

"Look," Dad said to Mum, "our daughter's of a superior race, and she needs to understand that. Otherwise, she'll be walked all over. These people are multiplying, they want to take over our country. Not if I have anything to say about it. We were talking down The Eagle the other day. Some black bastard's got your mate, Sally, pregnant. Bloody disgusting. Did you know?"

Mum turned and glared at him. "Yes, I knew. How about you see it from a different angle? That a new life's beginning?"

"Selfish, the pair of them. That kid's going to go through hell. It'll be brown, for fuck's sake, so everyone will know it's half and half. Who the hell willingly puts their kid through that?"

"Who the hell makes sure their kid is a racist? Silly me, I forgot, you're not included when it comes to being called out on things." Mum held the peeling knife up and jabbed it in the air. "What's it got to do with you what they're doing? Why can't you just let them be? Why do you and your mates think you have a say in who lives here and what they do?"

"Because it isn't right." Dad slurped some tea. "Anyway, less of your chatter and more of that

15

peeling, woman. I'm hungry. Been at work all fucking day. That food should have been ready as soon as I walked in. You've been slacking lately. I let it slide because you're working now, but it isn't on."

Mum glared at him and threw the knife in the sink. "Fucking make it yourself." She stalked over, took Faith's hand, and guided her out into the hallway. "Shoes on."

Faith obeyed, glancing back at Dad who gawped at them, his mouth open. The red spots on his cheeks meant he was angry. Faith swallowed, frightened in case he went off on one.

"Don't mind him," Mum said. "He's nothing but a bully. Just get a move on."

"Where do you think you're going?" Dad came to stand in the kitchen doorway, leaning on the frame, his fists clenched.

"To a place where the air doesn't stink. Somewhere I can breathe."

"What about my grub?"

"Like I said, make it yourself."

"You ought to watch your mouth, Nell."

Mum spun to face him. "Is that another of your threats? I'm telling you, they don't wash with me. I'm not afraid of you now, got that? You're pathetic, can only get by when you're controlling others. Take a good look at yourself, remember what you did."

"Aww, boring! Stop dragging that up."

"I'll drag up whatever the fuck I like, thank you. I told you last week, you're not the boss of me. I want you out. A divorce. I'm not putting up with this anymore."

"You'll regret it if you walk out," he said.

"I doubt it."

"Don't think you're coming back here after you've stormed off. I pay the rent. This is my place."

"Both our names are on the tenancy, and I pay the rent now, or had you forgotten?"

"That job of yours… You've changed since you started there."

"For the better."

"Think what you're doing."

"I am."

Outside, Mum led the way down the street, past Mrs Peters who stood on her doorstep, giving Mum a nod.

"I heard you shouting," the woman said. "About time you put him in his place. Good for you. That's been a long time coming."

"Too right," Mum said.

Faith rushed alongside her, gripping her hand tight. The sun shone, the early evening bringing kids out to play on the road. The end of September still dragged summer along behind it, not wanting to let go.

They reached the chippy on the corner, the windows fogged, ghostly figures of people beyond the glass. Mum stepped in, Faith right behind her, wet heat from the fryer steam coating her face. Mum bought enough for four people and held the brown paper bag close to her chest as she marched out.

Faith followed. Where were they going? It was the opposite direction to home. A few turns later, Faith's legs hurting from trying to keep up, they stood in front of a red door. Mum knocked, glancing up and down the street as if waiting for Dad to turn up.

A woman answered. Blonde, pretty, and tall, she smiled, then a frown bunched her forehead. "Nell? What are you doing here?"

"I've brought dinner."

"Oh. Ours is in the oven so…"

Mum sighed. "Can it save until tomorrow?"

"Well, yeah, but…"

"Good. I had to get out. James is being a prick."

"Again?" The woman moved back to let them in. "What's he done this time?"

"You don't want to know."

Faith trailed them down a dark, dingy hallway. It gave her the creeps, and the air smelled of sausages mixed with something she couldn't identify. They entered the kitchen. It wasn't like the one at home. This one had a couple of wonky cupboard doors, and the lino curled up at the corner of the base units, a dried pea hiding beneath the overhang. While it appeared tidy, the disrepair gave it a dirty feel all the same. Dad would say the people who lived here were down on their uppers and ought to work harder to get more money.

"Clinton will be home from work in a minute..." The lady wrung her skinny hands.

Mum raised her eyebrows. "So? You know me better than that, Sally."

Faith felt a little sick. Sally. The one who was pregnant by—

"Can I go home?" Faith said.

"No." Mum pressed Faith's shoulders so she sat at the table. "You're going to learn a thing or two, young lady. Not everything your father tells you is the truth."

Sally eyed Mum funny. "Are you thinking of using Clinton to make a point? Like he's some kind of bloody show pony?"

"What?" Mum shook her head. "No! I want Faith to understand how lovely he is, that's all. She needs this. How can I help her see without her being introduced to him?"

Sally lowered to a chair and rested her elbows on the table. "Sorry, it's just I'm so aware of what he goes through. I get protective."

"Understandable," Mum said. "Now, where's your plates, or do you want to wait until Clinton comes back? The chips and fishcakes should stay warm for a while yet."

A key scraped in the lock, and Faith turned to stare down the hallway. A giant black man in a blue boilersuit closed the door, and her stomach rolled over. Dad would go mad if he knew she was here with 'one of them'. She wanted to run, but it would mean going past him. He was a monster, he didn't belong in this country, and she was supposed to get as far away from his sort as possible.

"I..."

"Stay where you are," Mum warned. "Don't you dare move."

Fearing for her backside once Dad discovered where they'd been, Faith bowed her head, tears stinging. Mum got up. Out of the corner of her eye, Faith watched the scene unfold. Mum hugged Clinton — she hugged a black man! — and Clinton laughed.

"I smell chips," he said.

Faith looked up.

Clinton caught her movement and smiled down at her. "And who's this lovely young lady?"

Mum widened her eyes at Faith for her to be polite.

Uncomfortable, scared, and worried, Faith mumbled her name.

"Beautiful," Clinton said. "That's my mother's name." He ruffled her hair.

She recoiled. Oh God, he'd touched her.

"Nell's brought us dinner." Sally walked to a cupboard and took mismatched plates out.

"That's very nice of you," Clinton said. "Thank you."

He seemed all right. Kind, jolly, and his smile was so big and his clothes so clean he couldn't be any of the words Dad would call him, could he? Scum, filth.

Everyone but Clinton sat. He went to the sink and washed his hands, took his boilersuit off to reveal jeans and a T-shirt, then poured four glasses of Corona pop. Cherryade. Bottle empty, he screwed the lid on. "You can take the bottle back and keep the money, Faith."

Dad never let her do that. She always had to hand the pop money over.

"What do you say, Faith?" Mum prompted.

"Thank you." Faith felt weird. Dad had told her she didn't have to be nice to people like Clinton, that they were beneath her, but she wasn't sure what that meant. All she did know was to avoid them, to stay with her own kind, and if he knew she'd taken the bottle back to the shop and kept the money… Unsure what to do, she burst out crying.

"What's the matter?" Clinton asked. "Are you all right, honey?"

"She's fine." Mum kicked Faith's ankle under the table. "Hasn't been herself lately."

The urge to run came back, so strong it seemed it was alive inside her, a real thing pushing for her to stand and get out. But her food, placed in front of her by Sally, occupied Faith; she concentrated on cutting the fishcake into pieces.

"Will you be in trouble for coming here?" Clinton asked Mum.

"I don't care if I am."

"I know, but…"

"Let me worry about that."

"But what if he comes round? Takes it out on me?"

"He won't. I know things about him. He wouldn't dare."

Faith had heard this before. Her parents rowing, Dad laying down the law, Mum saying if he kept on, she'd tell all and sundry what he'd done. Faith didn't know what that was, but it must be bad because he always backed down.

Life was full of uncertainty and mixed messages. It left her with a constant sore belly, and she wanted to be sick sometimes. Would Mum remind Dad she had the 'upper hand' as she put it, when he found out they'd eaten dinner with a black man? That she'd spent her hard-earned money on Clinton? And what about the divorce? What would happen then?

Faith continued eating, listening to Clinton's tales of St Thomas, told to him by his mother. He wanted to visit one day but couldn't afford it, maybe never would. A walk on the white beach, the ocean slapping at his feet. Listening to music created on the steel pan—apparently a drum—played at one of the carnivals. It all sounded so happy, this place he described, and colourful.

She hoped he could go there.

No, she hoped he could never go there, that's what Dad would want her to think.

The war waged, the opposing sides battling for prominence. Dad and his ways, his beliefs, Clinton and his amazing stories, his booming laugh, and his offer to nip to the shop to buy Faith some cola bottle sweets for pudding.

She cried again, overwhelmed with the conflict inside her.

"Pack it in," Mum hissed when Sally and Clinton cleared the plates away. "Do you see how wrong your dad is now? Do you?"

Yes, Faith saw it, but it didn't mean it was right, being here.

She could only hope Dad never found out.

Chapter Three

Austin shouldn't be fucking about on Whitehall turf, the same as he shouldn't have fucked about on Cardigan, but he'd done both. A fan of gambling, he'd been a frequent visitor at Jackpot Palace, the twins' casino down the road. He'd lost a lot, and he owed a lot. The loan shark's bully boys, from The Judas Estate, had been putting pressure on him. He'd borrowed ten grand on a night he'd been pissed as a fart, lamenting the fact his wife had left him months before, taking their two kids with her. Stupidly, he'd gone to the shark so he could go on a gambling bender, his drunk brain convinced he'd win thousands.

He hadn't.

Counselling didn't help as much as he'd hoped, although he hadn't been to Jackpot Palace for a while, so maybe it had. George had sent him to their therapist, Vic, an old boy who'd tried to fix Austin's anger issues. Not that Austin had chosen to go down that route, he'd been forced.

He'd helped Goldie recently, before the leader had gone missing, by turning a blind eye when Goldie had shot some woman outside his house. George and Greg had paid a visit to ask why he'd done it, why he hadn't told them instead. Austin had been in a particularly bad place mentally, twitching and rude, tired, and George had got arsey. In the end, George had gone soft and sent him to Vic who hadn't come up with a magic wand to spirit all of his troubles away. They were still there, bar the actual gambling. He still thought about it a lot, though.

And it hadn't solved the issue about the money. Benny Bender, as he was called behind his back, lent money to anyone and everyone; no checks, nothing. So long as you agreed to pay it back, you were golden. And Austin *had* agreed, at a rate he could afford out of his wages once all the bills had been paid and he'd handed over child support. But now Benny wanted more, he'd changed the goalposts two weeks ago, and Austin was getting desperate. He didn't have the extra five hundred a month to spare, but he had to fork it out by the end of this week. He had to pay it, because he didn't want Benny doing what he was best at—bending fingers back until they snapped.

Austin had left Faith Lemon alone once he'd told her what he needed her to do, expecting her to do it soon, to have understood the urgency. Days had passed, him going to the wheelie bin to check it, finding fuck all. Then he'd heard about her son being murdered and had the decency to let her mourn. She hadn't replied until today. It was probably just as well. He'd been drunk when he'd written it, threatening to strangle her. Jesus Christ, he couldn't strangle *anyone*, but she wasn't to know that. He'd been mean to her when he'd approached her to do the job, desperation turning him into someone he didn't like.

He'd chosen her because of her age, thinking she'd be afraid to refuse. She hadn't been scared at all, had shouted right in his face. To get her down off her high horse, he'd said he'd let everyone know what she did for a living. That had sealed the deal. The fear in her eyes over that… It seemed she wanted to keep her East End rep intact, one of a gobby cow who'd swallowed too many bitter pills. The shame of them knowing how she earned her money was clearly something she didn't want to suffer.

He had to ensure Satin watched Faith when she rolled up at work, get her to keep him in the loop. Satin, an old school friend, one he'd bumped into when he'd gone into Whitehall's sex shop, wasn't who she appeared. At the time, he'd been spying on his wife, Maxine, to see what she was up to, thinking she'd left him for another bloke and was buying some sexy underwear. Hiding behind a rack of vibrators hadn't exactly been the best place to see an old mate for the first time in years, and Satin had gathered he didn't want attention drawn to him. She'd taken him through the back to the storage area, and they'd got chatting. Everything had tumbled out, and she'd suggested the money in the safe upstairs.

He'd been that anxious about Benny, he'd gone along with it.

How the fuck had it come to this? How had his life changed so much? He'd thought his marriage was solid, that he'd be with Maxine for life, but no, it had all gone tits up. Now, here he was, eager to pay Benny off in full so he could get his act together and start again.

He *did* have an option, though, one he wouldn't take unless the theft went wrong. The twins. Would they give him that much? Or would Sienna, their lender, part with so much dosh? And would George and Greg expect him to do something for them as well as repaying the money? Austin wasn't a beefy sort, he didn't like violence, although he'd done a good job of pretending he did with Faith. What if The Brothers expected him to kill for them?

They won't give you the time of day anyway, so why are you thinking about it?

Maybe he could go back to Prince on The Judas Estate, like he had when Benny had sent some fella round again last week to remind him that if he ever reneged on his payments, he'd find himself dead. Jesus, he'd agreed to pay it back, so why all the menacing tactics? Prince had laughed him out of the pub where they'd met up, saying Benny was a legitimate lender, had his approval, and it was up to Austin to abide by the rules.

Rules he hadn't known about. He'd never have taken the money if he'd known he was going to be asked to pay more than the agreed amount.

Stuck between a rock and a hard place, he reckoned the theft was the way to go for now. If Faith let him down, he'd have to think about what to do next. She'd do it, she *had* to, and everything would be okay. Satin had told him this woman, Vanda, would be the prime suspect because she was always skint and moaning about having to pay out for this and that, her three adult kids rinsing her on the daily. He had to have hope that Satin would oversee everything going on inside the brothel and keep her mouth shut once they had the spoils in their hands. As for Faith…if she got the wobbles once the job was done, he'd have to get nastier, something he didn't want to do.

He was playing a big boys game when he was just a toddler.

What was it she'd said? He checked the message string again. Fucking Nora, her face being slashed could be for a number of reasons. Who had she pissed off? Or was it something to do with Lemon? Had one of his cronies nipped round to warn her to keep her trap shut about something? No one had seen any of them around lately, though…

AUSTIN: WHO SLASHED YOUR FACE?

FAITH: WHY DO YOU NEED TO KNOW?

AUSTIN: BECAUSE IT COULD AFFECT WHAT WE'RE DOING.

FAITH: SOME SCOTTISH BLOKE CAME ROUND. GINGER FELLA. SAID HE WAS FROM THE BROTHERS.

Oh God. Austin *really* didn't need those two in the mix.

AUSTIN: WHAT THE FUCK DID YOU DO?

FAITH: I WAS HORRIBLE TO SOMEONE, AND THE TWINS FOUND OUT.

AUSTIN: IS IT OVER? I MEAN, THEY WON'T BE SENDING HIM ROUND AGAIN?

FAITH: I BLOODY HOPE NOT. LOOK, I'M ON THE BUS, ALMOST AT MY STOP, SO GO AWAY.

AUSTIN: TELL ME WHEN THE CASH IS IN THE BIN.

He slid his phone in his pocket and walked into his kitchen. It could do with a good scrub, but with work as a taxi driver, seeing Vic, and nipping to visit the kids every evening for an hour, he didn't get much spare time. Maxine would have a fit if she saw it like this. The house had been her dream home, and even though they rented it, they were allowed to make changes. Put up shelves and pictures, stuff like that. She'd spent a lot of time on it, the landlord not fussed so long as it enhanced the property, and Austin had let it go to rack and ruin. Probably because it would hurt Maxine—he'd done a lot of things to hurt her when they'd first spilt. Now, he imagined her calling him a pig.

As it was his day off, he got on with cleaning, doing a week's worth of crusty washing up and cursing himself for being such a slob. It brought home how much he'd let Maxine deal with on her own when they'd been a couple. The house, the kids, her part-time job while the children were at school. He'd acted as if he was lord of the fucking manor and she was his skivvy. He deserved to be left all on his tod. She, on the other hand, deserved a bloke who'd treat her like a princess.

Why had he allowed things to get this far? Not the lack of cleaning, but his marriage. Why had he assumed they were unbreakable? With her walking out, only taking clothes and personal possessions, setting up home down by The Angel, his life had imploded. The alcohol. The gambling. The sheer stupidity of stalking her and getting caught. She'd really gone to town on him then, a load of verbal smacking him in the face. He was amazed he could see the kids every day, considering how he'd behaved.

She was worth a million of him.

I'll get Benny paid off then sort myself out, I swear.

He cleaned the rest of the house to take his mind off what Faith was—or wasn't—doing. She would contact him if the money was in the wheelie bin—something he should have insisted on earlier, seeing as he'd fished in there day after day with no results. *That* had told him he wasn't cut out for this sort of thing. If he couldn't even get the basics right, he had no chance.

That's what came of your wife doing all the thinking for you. Maxine was a whiz at organisation, the house, the finances, life in general. He was lost without her, but there was no getting her back now. He'd confessed about the gambling, how quickly it had become an addiction, and she'd held her hand up to stop him talking.

"You know how I feel about that," she'd said. "My dad all but ruined my childhood because of the slot machines, so if you think I'll let you do the same to our kids, you've got another think coming."

He should never have confided in her but, as usual, he'd thought he'd have got away with it. You know, she'd have seen him crying, seen he'd meant every word about being a better person, and would agree to come home. Help him.

"Shit!"

Annoyed with his inadequacies, plus how he thought he could oversee a robbery and get away with it, he kicked Henry Hoover into the cupboard under the stairs and slouched off to make a coffee. An orderly house was meant to create an orderly mind, but he was fucked if it had calmed him down. If anything, his nerves had scrunched so tight his limbs had gone tense.

Coffee sorted, he checked his phone. Nothing from Faith. Should he contact Satin?

He sat in the living room and stared out the front. A car pulled up across the road where the nosy old biddy lived, and two men got out.

"Aww, fucking hell. What *now*?"

Had Faith gone running to them and grassed him up? They *knew* he worked during the day, so why come now? Had they been watching him to know he was home? Mind you, it wasn't like they'd care about his schedule. If they wanted to see him, they'd fucking well see him.

He got up and went to the door, not giving them a chance to knock. "Everything all right?"

George raised his eyebrows. "That's what we've come to check, plus something else. Get the kettle on."

He pushed past and walked into the kitchen. Greg followed, leaving Austin standing there, trembling.

How many people can just walk into a house and get away with it like that?

He shut the door, collected his coffee from the living room, and joined them. George had made himself at home, clean cups taken out of the cupboard, pouring boiled water into them. Greg went to the fridge and lifted the milk out, handing it to him.

Austin stared. He had no say in what they did, and it rubbed him up the wrong way. It seemed the whole of his life was governed by other people doing whatever the fuck they liked.

He kept his mouth shut on that, though. Didn't fancy a punch in the face. "Err, so you're here to what, check whether I've been seeing Vic?"

"We know you have." George added coffee granules, then sugar and milk. "Seems he's had a good effect. The house is nice and clean. It was a shit state last time we were here. Stank like a dirty arsehole."

"Yeah, well, it needed doing." Austin sat at the little table, placing his cup on a coaster. Maxine would have liked that. "I've been to see him every week, so…"

"We know that an' all." George smiled and passed his brother a coffee. "Funny enough, we tend to keep abreast of things. How's tricks?"

Austin's skin went clammy. *Were* they here because of Faith? Were they feeling him out to see if he slipped up? Toying with him?

"Same old. Work, kids, nothing special."

"What do you want out of life?" Greg leaned his backside against the sink unit. "Is this it, what you have? Got any ambitions?"

To pay off Benny Bender and get my act together. "Nah, I've never been one to reach for the stars."

"Maybe that's why Maxine left you," George said.

Of *course* they'd know her name. They'd probably looked into him after the Goldie fiasco. Maybe they *had* been watching him. Shit, would they have seen him ferreting in the wheelie bin?

For the lack of something to say, he blurted, "Vic's been teaching me to think before I speak."

"Good, because you were fucking rude before, hence seeing him for anger management." George sipped. "I mean, you had some balls to speak to me the way you did."

Austin preferred not to remember that, thanks. Especially the bit where George had him around the throat. "I haven't got arsey for a while now." He'd lied, he'd kicked Henry Hoover, but maybe that didn't count.

"Good." Greg cocked his head. "We've got a job for you."

"How much does it pay?" He hadn't meant to say that, had never been good at keeping his foot out of his mouth.

"Having money troubles, are you?" George asked.

"You could say that."

"Oh dear. Anything we can help with?"

Yeah. Got ten grand knocking about, have you?
"Nah, I just need to earn more. The monthly bills going up…"

"It's happening to everyone." George sighed. "Gets right on my tits. How are people meant to eat?"

Did he expect an answer? Austin could never tell whether something was rhetorical or not. "Dunno."

"Back to the job," Greg said. "Are you interested if the money's right?"

"Yeah, but… Why me?"

Greg smiled. "You're George's next project."

"Eh?"

"He feels sorry for certain people, wants to help them, and you're the current subject. Just be grateful."

"Um, okay?"

"So how much are we talking?" Greg asked. "What do you need?"

"Five hundred a month to get myself straight, although I've got a monkey on my back, hammering down the door. I need it by the end of the week." He wouldn't have to resort to the robbery if he earned Benny's extra payment. He could tell Faith not to bother.

"Who the fuck wants that much off you?" George barked. "Are you in proper bother?"

"Nah, I'm just behind on one bill, that's all. They want the last two payments I missed else I'll be taken to court." That had sounded plausible, hadn't it?

"Rent?"

"No, it's…" He couldn't tell them. Irritation surged. "Look, does it matter?"

George shrugged. "Suppose not, but watch your tone."

"Sorry. I get wound up easy, that's all."

"So we heard. Maxine said you have a short temper. Maybe you should go and see Vic twice a week instead."

Austin didn't like them finding out about him through Maxine. It was a violation of his privacy, wasn't it? She had a negative view of him, so whatever she told them would be tainted.

But what can you do about it, dickhead? They're The Brothers.

"So, the job?" He swigged some coffee, told himself to calm down. This could be the windfall he'd been praying for.

"You're a taxi driver." George smiled. "No one would take any notice of you. We need you to deliver a package to The Whitehall Estate tonight."

Austin's guts went south. Was George fucking with him to see his reaction by mentioning that estate? "Whitehall?"

"Yeah, to Mrs Whitehall's house."

Oh God, is she going to be waiting with her henchmen when I go? Is this all a trap? They know what I've got planned? "Depends what's in the package."

"Drugs."

He hadn't expected that. He'd thought it would be bodies or something. "Shit, so I take all the risk of being pulled over and you don't."

"That's about the long and short of it." George grinned. "We've taken over where the Sparrow Lot left off. Got gear surplus to our requirements as we've agreed to keep buying off the people the Sparrows did so they're not left in the lurch—there's only so many drugs we want floating around on our patch. Mrs Whitehall's taking it off our hands. It'll be a weekly thing."

"How much per trip?"

"Five hundred."

Austin totted that up. Two grand on a four-week month, two and a half for a five. He'd have Benny paid off in no time. "I'll do it."

"Good boy." George grinned again. "You know it makes sense."

Chapter Four

George walked into their latest acquisition, a gastro pub called Noodle and Tiger. While it served posh nosh, you could also buy a chicken and mushroom Pot Noodle with slices of tiger bread topped with Anchor butter, although he was also partial to Lurpak. He was hungry so had come here for his favourite food instead of going all the way home.

Nessa, the woman who ran it for them, was the daughter of one of Ron Cardigan's older bully boys, Dickie Feathers, formally known as the Beast in the days he'd worked for Ron. She flashed a toothy smile, tucked a stray lock of hair behind one ear, and came to serve them. "The usual grub?"

George nodded. "A Coke an' all, thanks."

Greg asked for the same plus a ham and piccalilli doorstep sandwich.

George looked around. The place was packed, as had been his dream, and he gave himself a pat on the back. People might be skint, but they still wanted a meal out. The prices were as low as they could get them (the drinks brought in the profits), so the residents had somewhere to eat upmarket food that didn't hurt their pockets too much. All part of his 'do good' mission, to give back to a community that, for the most part, was loyal to them.

Their mother would have been proud.

"I knew this place would work," he said to Greg.

A roll of the eyes, and Greg nodded. "Yeah, you said before."

"You were ready to veto it, though."

"I was wrong, all right? Fuck me, could you get any smugger?"

"I can do if you like."

"Bog off."

They took their drinks to a corner and sat, George's back to the wood-panelled wall so he could see the whole place, admire their new domain.

"What did you make of Austin?" he asked.

Greg pursed his lips. "I knew that visit was bugging you. Why didn't you say something in the car on the way here?"

"I was mulling it over, seeing if I was being a twat in suspecting there's something up. What d'you reckon?"

"He seemed cagey about needing money. Didn't want to say who he owed."

"Hmm, that's what got my attention."

George smiled at the waitress coming with their food. He'd given explicit instructions as to how much water went into his Pot Noodle, glad the chef had got it right.

He waited for the woman to walk away and said, "I bloody love these."

"You'll turn into a noodle if you're not careful."

"Better than turning into that yellow shit you've got in your sarnie. You've been eating a lot of that this past week."

"Fuck me, keeping an eye on me much?"

They ate, George watching the customers. Many had money, it was clear from their clothes, but others appeared skint. For the first time he worried this pub and all the advertising they'd done hadn't been such a good idea after all. What if people were coming here, robbing Peter to pay Paul in order to eat at what was rapidly becoming 'the place to be'? FOMO might be playing a part in them walking through those doors.

A mother and her child sat three tables away. George knew the mum in a roundabout way, she was on benefits, and a twinge of guilt prodded him at possibly contributing to her lack of cash by encouraging her to come here. He'd mentioned the Noodle and Tiger to her last week. Her baby was about six months old and well cared for, so she clearly looked after him; maybe she knew how to make the pennies stretch.

"Shit."

"What?" Greg asked.

"Hang on." George fished one of his usual envelopes out of his inner suit jacket pocket and casually walked over to her table. "All right?"

Anna looked up. Blonde and blue-eyed, she appeared about twenty-five. "Oh, hello…"

"I forgot to give you this last week. You know, when I saw you on the market."

She stared at the envelope he held out. "Err, what's that for?"

"Something for the nipper." He returned to his table and folded a thick slice of tiger bread in half, dipping it into his noodle pot.

"What the fuck was that about?" Greg asked.

"Felt sorry for her."

"You can't go feeling sorry for everyone, bruv."

"Whatever."

George thought about Becky and Noah. She'd been skint until they'd helped her out recently. Why should they squirrel away all their wealth when there were so many people to help? The profits from their casino alone amounted to a big wedge, not to mention everything else they dabbled in.

Becky had settled well in Southend, leaving her miserable East End life behind, and George had been instrumental in setting up a trust fund for Noah. That little family of two had tugged at his heartstrings. Greg had fallen in love with Noah, and he wanted that kid to have a good start in his adult life.

Maybe they ought to poke around about Anna, see what her true situation was. She could maybe work for them.

He got up again.

"Where are you going *now*?" Greg asked. "Your noodles are going to get soggy, and you know how much that pisses you off. I'm not in the right frame of mind to deal with you in that sort of mood."

George ignored him and sat at Anna's table. "Tell me about yourself."

She stared at him. "Um, what?"

"I'm not playing at speed dating, love. Just answer me. What did you do before you had the baby?"

"Hairdressing."

George resisted punching the air. Was Mum looking down on them, sending him in the right direction? "Any good, are you?"

"I'm all right."

"Need a job?"

"I'd love one, but childcare costs will take most of my wages, so what's the point?"

"What if childcare wasn't a problem?"

"Err..."

He lowered his voice. "Say me and my brother have got this salon we've not long bought and renovated. Say we need a manager and there's a room out the back where your boy can sleep. You could put him in a playpen in the shop when he's awake. Would you be interested?"

She eyed him warily. "What's the catch?"

"Smart woman, because there's *always* a catch." He glanced round to check for listening ears. "*Things* will be stored there."

"What things?"

He leaned forward. "The guns we use." He didn't add the bit about the drugs.

She reared back, her face flushing, and busied herself handing the baby a fat chip. "I don't...I don't want to be involved in anything like that."

"You don't have to do anything dodgy, you'd just let our people in through the back. They'd have to have a password, but you get the gist. The lease was up for the place we used so we needed a new gaff. There's a flat upstairs. You can have it, rent-free."

She stared at him.

George sighed. "Okay, if you're not interested, just keep your mouth shut about this conversation. If word gets out you blabbed, I'll know it was you because I haven't discussed this with anyone else."

She blinked. "I wouldn't dare say anything anyway."

"I know, that's why I'm sitting here."

"I…" She clamped her mouth shut.

"Look, you'd run the hairdresser's and keep an eye on the place, might get a knock on the door in the middle of the night, but that's it."

"How much?"

Got you. "A grand a week. You'd have to give up the benefits. You know how some people will see you working and grass you up. Cash in hand, though, so it's up to you if you pay your taxes. They're fuck all to do with us."

Her eyes bulged. "A grand? What happens when my baby gets too old? He'll be running around, being a pest. There's scissors and everything."

"You'd be able to afford to get him into a nursery. What's his name anyway?"

"Harper."

"Dad fucked off, did he?"

"One-night stand. I don't even know who he is."

George detected a lie there but wouldn't pry. She knew damn well who the father was, she just didn't want to say. "Then you need all the help you can get."

She bit her bottom lip. "What if the shop gets raided by the police?"

"Then you'll say you had no idea that behind one of the walls is a secret panel. You just run the place, know what I mean?"

"I don't know, it's all a bit…a bit illegal."

He laughed. "Most things to do with me and my brother are. Have a think."

Anna nodded. Stared at the card. Looked at her baby, then at him. "I'll do it."

George smiled. "Thought you might. Send me your number, and I'll get back to you on the details later. In the meantime…" He took out another envelope, a thicker one. "Have that."

He returned to his twin, even ate some of his soggy noodles and didn't piss and moan about it.

"What are you up to?" Greg asked.

"I've found our hairdresser."

"Have you offered her the job without getting her checked out first?"

George shrugged. "Might have done."

"For fuck's *sake*, when will you learn?"

"She's skint, needs a break."

"But she could be a danger to us."

"Then we'll poke around before she starts, all right? No need to get your knickers in a twist."

Greg scowled. "You're a bloody nightmare."

George smiled. "I know."

But he had a good feeling about Anna, right from when they'd chatted in the market. She was a good girl, he knew it, otherwise he wouldn't have approached her.

He sent a message to get a couple of their men to go and ask questions. By the end of the day, they'd know everything they needed to about her.

Chapter Five

*I*n her bedroom, the door open, Faith covered her ears. Dad shouted at Mum downstairs, his voice carrying. It was so loud she had no trouble picking up their row.

"Who the fuck do you think you are, leaving me to cook my own dinner?" he barked.

"Who the fuck do you think you are, believing a woman's place is chained to the kitchen sink even when she goes to work? Times are changing, women know they've got rights."

"Where have you been?"

"None of your business."

"Our Faith will tell me, so you may as well say."

"Leave Faith alone. She's a child and doesn't deserve to hear your drivel."

"Drivel! What you call drivel is the truth, woman. I'm just educating her so she can stand up for herself against the others."

"The others? Christ, you're the one who needs educating."

"Where. Did. You. Go?"

"To the chippy, all right? Now sod off out of my face."

"Where did you eat your dinner?"

"For God's sake! I haven't answered to you for months, and no amount of wheedling on your part will make me change my mind now. I deserve a voice, to have a say in what goes on in my life."

"Maybe this will shut you up, then."

Mum screamed, and something clattered. A kitchen chair falling over?

"That's the last fucking time you'll do that to me, James Wilson," Mum said.

"Or what? Come on, tell me what you're going to do if I wallop you again."

"Do you really need to ask?"

Footsteps. Out in the hallway.

"Faith!" Mum called. "Come down here, please."

Faith scrambled from her bed in her pyjamas and rushed to the top of the stairs.

"You're not taking her anywhere. She belongs with me." Dad gripped Mum's arm and spun her to face him. "If she goes with you, fuck knows what shit you'll pump into her head."

"If she stays with you, she'll grow up racist." Mum glanced up and shook off Dad's hold. "Quickly now, Faith. We have to go out."

Faith gasped. Mum had a black eye.

"Where are you going?" Dad shoved a hand through his hair.

"I did warn you. One more episode, and I was telling all."

"No, Nell. Not that."

Mum jammed her hands on her hips. "How many chances do you need to realise I'm serious? I said if you hit me again, that was it. I said if you tried to influence Faith anymore, that was it. But you know best, always have, and thought you could push it and I wouldn't do anything. Well, you're wrong. Now fuck off out of my face."

Dad slumped against the wall, his shoulder skewing a picture frame. "Anything but that. Anything. I'll move out. We'll get a divorce like you want. I won't bother you anymore."

"Too late."

Faith moved down the stairs, nervous, unsure what to do. Go with Mum or stay with Dad? She loved them both and didn't know which one she'd be better off with. Would she have to cook and clean if it was just her and Dad? And where would they go if she went with Mum? Why wasn't Mum packing a suitcase? Faith didn't want to leave all her things behind. The stuffed animals, her Sindy doll. Her collection of Whimsies, the little ornaments she'd placed on her bedside table; the giraffe, camel, tiger, and wolf.

Her stomach hurt again.

"Shoes," Mum said. "And your coat. We'll probably be out late."

So they were coming back? Faith felt a bit better about that, so she stuck her shoes and coat on and waited by the front door, hands in pockets.

"You either make a run for it or stay, makes no odds to me," Mum said to Dad. "It's best I don't know where you're going if you do bolt. If I don't know, I can't tell them."

"Nell, for God's sake, don't do this."

Mum shoved her arms in her coat sleeves then straightened the fronts. She hung her bag on her shoulder and stared him in the eye. "What you need to learn is that the tide is turning. Women don't have to put up with this shit, and neither do a lot of other people. You're twisted, sick in the head, and I should have done something about this years ago. You've got away with it for too long. I'm not your punchbag, nor am I willing to let you walk away scot-free from what you did that horrible night."

Horrible night?

Dad groaned. Normally, he'd be shouting, telling Mum she ought to shut up, but for some reason, tonight he seemed different. Was he scared? Did he want to hit Mum again but couldn't risk it?

"I'll be finished," he said.

"Good. Maybe you'll finally learn your lesson in the nick."

Mum grabbed Faith's hand and herded her onto the street. The front door slammed, but Mum paid it no mind. She marched along the pavement, Faith running to keep up, her chest hurting, her eyes stinging. The nick? That meant prison. What had Dad done? Mum *must have kept it a secret. Was she telling on him because he'd hit her? Faith had grown up knowing about the punches but had never seen him thump her. Still, bruises didn't lie, did they, and it didn't take much for her to work out he hit and slapped her. Mum used to be frightened of him, but lately she'd been chatting back, standing up for herself since she'd started work at the factory down by The Eagle.*

"Where are we going?" Faith asked.

"The police station."

"Why?"

"Because I have something to tell them."

"Like what?"

"Something I should have told them years ago."

"What's that?"

"Never you mind. Just know your father isn't a nice man. I never should have married him. How could I have been so stupid? Anyway, that's enough of that. Come on, we've got a way to go yet."

Faith trotted beside her, the cool evening air fresh in her nose. How long would they be at the police station? There was school tomorrow, and Faith didn't want to miss it. Mrs Collins had promised they could bake cakes. Mum had bought all the ingredients, weighing it out and putting it in little Tupperware pots earlier.

"You might have to stay off school," Mum said. "But I'll call in sick at work and bake the cakes with you, all right?"

It wouldn't be the same, but it was better than nothing.

Faith trudged on, her chest heavy, her eyes sore from the tears that spilled.

Sometimes, she wished she'd never been born.

Mum sat at a table in a bare-walled room, dark scuff marks ruining the white paint. Faith, on the floor in the corner with a book and a can of Coke, had been told to read it while Mum spoke to the officers. That or go into another room with a social worker. Mum had said no, she wanted Faith near her, no matter that she might hear what she had to say.

An old man with grey hair called Detective Bassett sat opposite Mum with another policeman who'd said he was a sergeant. Smith. He had a uniform on, and it scared Faith. She didn't like coppers. Dad said they were the scourge of the earth, only out there to collar you; they didn't really want to help, just said it so they looked good. Bassett had a notepad, and Smith had a form on a clipboard which he'd filled out at the top.

Faith dipped her head. The book, about a dragon and a princess, was one she'd wanted to read, but the words kept blurring. She pretended to be engrossed, all the while listening.

"This is a very serious allegation, Mrs Wilson," Bassett said. "Are you sure you want to continue?"

"Yes. I wouldn't be here otherwise, would I."

"Despite the possible ramifications for you?"

"What do you mean?"

"Well, you've known about it for a long time. You didn't report it when it happened."

"Because he warned me if I did, he'd kill me, too."

"So what's changed in order for you to be here this evening?"

Faith looked up.

Mum straightened her spine. "I've grown a backbone, that's what. I started working at a factory, and you get to hear all sorts of opinions there, the main one that us women are sick of being walked over. See this?" She pointed to her black eye. "This is what I got because I didn't cook dinner. Should I stay at home and be the good little wife when this sort of shit happens? Am I being a decent role model for my daughter if I do? No, I'm bloody well not. It has to stop. If we don't stick up for ourselves, no one else will. So, what are these ramifications?"

Bassett cleared his throat. "Ah, well, if that's the way of it, then there might not be any. You've been coerced into keeping quiet, is that right?"

"Yes. What would happen if I hadn't?"

"You'd likely be classed as an accessory. You'd have to appear in court. Depending on your sentence, your daughter—"

"Fuck that." Mum stood. "I'll not be telling you anything in that case. There's no one who can take care of her without me or her father there. She's not going into care. Either you promise me I won't get done for anything, or I'm walking."

"In light of what you've said, I doubt you'll be in trouble."

"You doubt? But that's not a fact, is it? It's not a guarantee."

"Let me just have a word with my boss." Bassett left the room.

"Fucking ridiculous," Mum muttered and sat. "I couldn't say anything before because I was too scared, and now I've got the guts to do it, he threatens to take my kid away."

"It would be out of his hands," Smith said. "But he's a good man, he'll sort something out."

Silence descended. Faith managed a line about the dragon flying to rescue the princess from a tower. She wished she was that princess, that someone would come along and save her. Maybe that's what Mum was doing. If Dad had said he'd kill her for telling on him, perhaps he was a bad man. He didn't seem bad. Well, only when he shouted. All other times he cuddled her, bought her sweets. Taught her about the black people, the Indians, the Pakistanis and how they didn't belong.

She thought about the cola bottles Clinton had gone out to get for her. He must be a good man like Bassett, too.

More tears stung. More confusion.

Bassett came back and sat. "We'll take photos of that eye as proof of why you've been reticent to share what you know. My boss is happy that you've not been able to come down before now, so we'll just take your statement, then you can go home."

"Go home? How the hell can I do that? He'll know what I've done and beat the shit out of me. Oh, he might have seemed to accept that I was coming here, but don't let that fool you. He didn't actually believe I'd do it, and he'll be saving his fists for later. You lot need to go and arrest him before I set foot in there. And I still haven't got my guarantee," Mum said. "I want it in writing."

"We don't usually—"

62

She slapped the table. "I don't give a fuck what you usually do."

Bassett sighed and walked out again.

Faith stared at the book. The dragon poked its tail into the turret window, and the princess climbed on. The tail curled, and she was deposited on the dragon's back. They flew through the sky, soaring between clouds, off to a better life.

The detective returned. Placed a form in front of Mum. They talked quietly, low so Faith didn't pick up their words, but Mum seemed content now.

"Okay," Bassett said. "From the beginning, then."

Dad had killed a black man before Faith had been born. A drunken fight that had turned into murder. Faith understood it all, everything that had been said, but she couldn't imagine Dad doing that. He'd beaten the man up — Arvinda, his name was — and had walked away, stopping when Arvinda had called out, asking for help.

"Help?" Dad had said. "I'll give you fucking help."

He'd stamped on his head until his face was covered in blood. He'd grabbed Mum's arm and dragged her along the street, leaving Arvinda bleeding in the *darkness, Dad's mates jeering beside the body. Mum hadn't known he was dead at that point. It wasn't until it was in the evening paper the next day after someone had found Arvinda that morning.*

"He warned me if I said anything, I'd be next," Mum said.

"And you believed him?"

"Of course I bloody did! I was shit-scared of him."

"So why did you then go on to marry him?"

"You have no idea, do you? How men control. How I was forced into marriage because"—Mum glanced at Faith—"I was pregnant. My mother made me get married. The shame, all that rubbish. We're talking nineteen seventy-three here."

"I understand." Bassett pinched the bridge of his nose. "The other witnesses?"

"His mates, I told you that already."

"Could they have killed him? Is it possible your husband left him alive and his friends finished the job?"

"I don't know."

"Are you prepared to tell me their names?"

"Not likely. They're rough. Their families will come after me if they find out I grassed."

"We need more. At the moment, it's your word against his. Yes, you've given us your account, but as it was down a dark street…"

"So you're not going to do anything? Go round and speak to him, at least?"

"Oh yes, we'll pick him up, bring him here for questioning. Is he likely to crack under pressure?"

"Not at first, he'll deny it until he's blue in the face, but if you lean on him a bit, he'll cave in the end. My statement should be enough, surely. I was there, I saw him beat that man up. I've lived with this for years and still remember it plain as day."

"Right. Is there somewhere you can stay tonight? Give us a ring in the morning to check the state of play so you know if it's safe for you to go home?"

"I've got a friend. She might let us sleep on her sofa. I'll need to go home and collect a few bits and bobs first, though. Our nighties and whatever. I'll tell him we just went for a walk, that I didn't come here."

"That isn't wise. You've already said he'll be waiting to hit you."

"We're not kipping in our clothes!"

"Then we'll drop you off so we can keep an eye out."

"You are going to do something, aren't you? You're not going to sweep it under the rug because the man was black."

"Absolutely not. I was the first responder on that case. I've wanted to get my hands on the killer all this time. I assure you, I'll do everything I can to put your husband behind bars."

"You're not just saying that?"

"No. I promise."

Mum sighed. "Promises mean nothing. James promised he'd never be mean to a black person again, yet he still says things. He fills my daughter's head with crap."

"Best to distance yourself from him, then." Bassett glanced over at Faith. "All right there, love?"

Faith nodded. Except she wasn't all right and didn't think she ever would be.

Chapter Six

Faith entered the sex shop and smiled at the two cashiers. They glanced over and didn't give her a funny look, so she assumed her makeup had worked. Still, nerves waged a battle inside her, and she experienced being 'less than' or at least feeling that way.

It brought Becky to mind. It brought her nasty past to mind. And Reggie.

She forced herself to strut to the staff door like she usually would, head held high, that air of superiority about her, and weaved around customers. In the storeroom, she let her shoulders slump, took a deep breath, and mooched between the stacks of boxes and shelving to another door.

Shitty Sharon, as Faith privately called her, stood in the corner ripping open a box from a new delivery. She pulled out a red basque and held it up. "Fucking hell, get an eyeful of this."

Faith paused and stared over. The basque had a hole in the crotch. No stranger to the outfits, as she had to put them on to entertain customers, she shrugged. "Nice colour."

"Hmm, I think I'll have one of these." Shitty rooted around for her size.

Faith left her to it. She climbed the stairs to the brothel. In reception, she inhaled deeply again and glanced around. Three men sat waiting on the two black leather sofas, the leaf from a fake potted plant draping over one of their heads.

Too engrossed in his phone to care.

The scene reminded her of the first time she'd come here, for her interview. It had been so long ago. Another lifetime.

She smiled at blonde, twentysomething Petra behind the desk and approached, her stomach doing backflips.

Petra looked up. "Oh, bloody hell! I didn't expect to see *you* here yet." She studied Faith's face.

Faith squirmed. Could she see the scars? "I need to get back to work. I'm bored at home."

"I bet. Missed all those dicks, have you?"

"Err, no. The wages and the tips. I was only on sick pay."

"I get you. Okay, I'll let Mrs W know you're here."

One of the men stared Faith's way and grinned. "All right? Haven't seen you for a while. Are you back?"

She went over to him. Mike, about fifty, had shaved his head since she'd last seen him. He looked better without the monk-like hairdo.

"Hopefully." She didn't know what she'd do if she was sent home again. She *had* to rob that safe.

"Good," he said, "because I've missed you. I was put with Satin. Nice girl but not you. Know what I mean?"

She did. "Maybe I can see you today if Mrs Whitehall says I can."

"Why were you off anyway?" he asked.

Relieved her wrecked face didn't make it obvious, she said, "My son died."

"Shit, sorry to hear that."

She smiled. "I'd better go…"

She blinked back tears and moved towards the boss' office.

"Mrs W said to go straight in," Petra called out.

"Thanks," Faith said over her shoulder. She tapped as a courtesy then opened the door. Poked her head round.

Mrs Whitehall, sitting behind her marble desk, had dyed her hair strawberry blonde, and for moment it startled Faith. Her black eyeliner flew out in wings, her usual smoky-eye look going on. Her dark irises and pale lipstick gave her a starlet air. Mrs Whitehall was a few years older than Lemon, still young enough to appear fresh-faced. Faith felt dowdy by comparison.

"Come in," Mrs Whitehall said. "Sit down, and I'll get you a drink. Coffee? Or something stronger?"

"Coffee, please." Faith sat on the blue sofa to the left and placed her handbag on the low coffee table, marble to match the desk.

It was so weird being back here and feeling as if she no longer belonged. Maybe because she'd mentally checked out of this life and looked forward to the next elsewhere. At the same time, nostalgia hit her. The many years of working here, the smell of Mrs Whitehall's perfume, the ruse that this floor was for her office and the staff downstairs, yet off the reception, a hallway with many doors, behind which women worked, the accountant's office at the far end.

"To what do I owe the pleasure?" Mrs Whitehall poured from a carafe. "One sweetener, isn't it, and cream."

It had always unnerved Faith that the boss remembered how the employees took their drinks, amongst other things, as if she had a Rolodex in her mind containing all their information. "Yes. Thank you. Um, I'm ready to come back to work."

Mrs Whitehall brought two china cups over and put them on the table. She sat on the only armchair, a recliner, and perused Faith's face. "Lovely stitch work. That nurse needs a pay rise. I'll send her a little 'thank you' envelope if you tell me her name."

"Darla Quinn."

"Lovely. How are things otherwise?" Mrs Whitehall leaned back and crossed her slender legs.

"Lemon? Oh, you know, I'm getting by. The trouble is, I got used to him living with me again once he'd left Becky so…but I'll be all right."

"Do you know why your face was slashed?"

"Yes."

"And…?"

"The Brothers sent someone round."

Going by Mrs Whitehall's expression, she already knew. "Hmm. It must have been bad for them to do that."

"I was horrible to Becky. I deserved it. Couldn't see the wood for the trees, what with my dad and everything—I told you about him, didn't I. He fucked up my head. Still, it was on me, I could have opted not to speak to her that way, so I've only got myself to blame."

"It's humbling, isn't it, when we're faced with our downfalls. To own them is to grow."

Faith, although used to the woman's profound sayings, wasn't in the mood for them today. "I need to try harder. To watch my mouth."

"You've always been professional at work."

"I try to be."

"I'll overlook you annoying the twins this once, but if you do it again, upset my friends or anyone else, then I'll have to take measures of my own."

Faith's stomach rolled over. "I understand. Thank you." *If I get caught for stealing, she's going to go apeshit on me.*

"You can start straight away if you like," Mrs Whitehall said. "I see Mike's out there. He'll be pleased you're back. Satin isn't his cup of tea. Too young."

It hadn't been said as a barb, the insinuation that Faith was older, but she felt the sting of it anyway. "I've just spoken to him. He said similar."

Mrs Whitehall got up and walked to the door, opening it to call out, "Mike, you're with Faith now. Just give her twenty minutes to finish her coffee and get ready, okay?" She closed the door and returned to her chair. Picked up her cup and sipped. "Lemon's funeral. When is it?"

"I don't know. His body's still being kept as evidence. That's what the policewoman said."

"Ah yes. With a murder, they tend to hang on to it. Unfortunate business when they do that. Means the families can't move on with their mourning. A grieving soul is only half a person, their wings clipped for the duration."

Faith tamped down her irritation. Now wasn't the time for Mrs Whitehall to point out she was grieving, not when Faith had to appear to move on. Returning to work meant no baggage. She'd have to pretend to be happy. Laugh a lot. Maybe by pretending it might convince her that Lemon hadn't died. She could tell herself he'd just moved away. He wasn't dead, he'd chosen to start again elsewhere.

Faith sipped some coffee. "I'll get through it."

"I'm sure you will." Mrs Whitehall also sipped.

They sat quietly for a while, Faith's mind on getting in that safe and taking the money down to the wheelie bin. If she had her way, she'd remove her cut first—she had no idea whether she could trust Austin to pay her later—but having that cash on her if the shit hit the fan before she went home wouldn't be wise.

"When my husband died," Mrs Whitehall said, "I thought my life had ended. That I'd never laugh again—and when I did, I felt guilty. It seemed wrong to laugh when he was in the ground. But you have to fake it. People only have so much sympathy before they expect you to get on with things. You'll have to do that at work. The men won't want to have sex with a sourpuss."

"I've already thought the same."

"Of course you have. It doesn't hurt to reiterate it, though, does it. I have a business to oversee, after all, and I need it to run smoothly. Unhappy men means an unhappy bank account. Losing money isn't on my to-do list."

Losing money… She's going to lose a lot when I get my hands on it. Oh God. Annoyed by the subtle warning because it wasn't bloody necessary, Faith nodded. "I won't let you down."

"Make sure you don't. Your face won't look so good if *I* have to slash it." Mrs Whitehall rose and took her cup to the sideboard, her back to Faith. "And if I ever hear of you being racist again, I'll kill you."

Faith stood on shaky legs and managed to walk over to the boss and place her cup down. "I'm ashamed of myself. I was brought up wrong. It isn't too late to change, though."

Mrs Whitehall turned her head sideways to stare at her. "No, it isn't. You may go."

Faith left the office, glanced at Mike and smiled despite being unnerved, then went into her room, number six. In the shower, careful not to get her face or hair wet, she contemplated what Mrs Whitehall *hadn't* said. The twins must have got hold of her and told her why they'd had her face slashed. Why? Faith was their resident, so they didn't need permission to hurt her. Or was it because of her working on The Whitehall Estate and they wanted to warn her Faith might sling racial slurs at customers? She'd *never* done that here.

She got out and dressed in a floating negligee, light pink, and put on high-heeled fluffy slippers. Mike preferred the softer look, and she pondered, as she had in the past, whether his fondness for older women meant he had Mummy issues. The outfit certainly spoke of the nightwear from years ago.

She shuddered and pressed the buzzer. It alerted Petra that she was ready, and also the other way round, if a customer waited. She sat on the edge of the bed. This would become normal for her in the next few hours. Waiting. Hoping she had a clear run at the safe. Praying she didn't get caught.

Mike tapped on the door.

"Come in!" She fixed on a smile and told herself to keep it together. Soon, she could start her new life.

Better to focus on that than everything else.

Chapter Seven

Mrs India Whitehall looked out of her office window at the crappy view of another building, all red bricks, smut-laced from years ago when chimneys had belched out black smoke. It wasn't exactly a pleasurable sight, as blank and boring at it was, but she didn't want it to be a beautiful vista. No windows across the alley meant no chance of her being spied on. Her father had been wise choosing this shop.

She contemplated her recent conversation. Of *course* The Brothers had tipped her the wink about Faith and the way she'd treated Lemon's ex, Becky. The way she'd all but refused to have anything to do with her baby grandson because he had a black mother. India had never heard of Faith being racist while at work, but then she only had white customers so… If India ever heard it, she *would* kill her.

But I'm going to kill her for something else anyway…

She laughed. How delightful to have something to do other than running her sex business and all the other pies she had her fingers in. She enjoyed doing some damage as much as the next leader, letting people know *she* was the boss around here. Her penchant for bloodshed wasn't normal for a woman, she was well aware of that, but anger fuelled her most of the time, an anger that had followed her since her husband, Errol, had died, a shadow that wouldn't go away even in the darkness.

India kept her private life away from work. Barely anyone in her circle had met Errol when he'd been alive—he'd preferred being out of the limelight, and she'd shielded him because of what she did and who she was. He'd been precious to her, someone to wrap in cotton wool, and to draw attention to him, considering she was a fucking *gangster*, wouldn't have been wise. She couldn't risk him being killed to get back at her. People knew *of* him, and she was sure other leaders had spotted him from time to time if they'd been spying on her for whatever reason, but right up until the day he'd died of cancer, he'd been safe.

He'd also been black, so India had a score to settle on his behalf. Faith was the perfect whipping post, someone to take her grief out on because, Jesus Christ, India had never left the state of mourning. She appeared to be coping, and she used work to get by, but deep inside, hatred seethed. Hatred at the unfairness of life, how it had snatched Errol away from her too soon. They were supposed to retire together, go abroad and see out their days in a villa beside the beach, but his illness had other ideas.

Faith wouldn't know what had hit her. Not just for what she'd done to Becky and baby Noah, but for what she was about to do. Stealing wasn't on, it was treasonous, and Faith would soon see that fucking around on The Whitehall Estate would be her undoing.

India walked to her desk and picked up her burner phone. She pressed number one on speed dial and sat in her plush chair, crossing her legs. Satin answered after two rings.

India smiled. "She's here, so keep your eyes peeled. Let me know the second *he* makes contact."

"Will do."

Call cut, she clicked the CCTV footage button on her desktop, her monitor the curved kind, forty-nine inches. Numerous boxes appeared, of the shop and the stairwell, reception, the rooms. She selected Faith's. The cameras weren't there for her to spy on the sex acts, she wasn't a bloody deviant, but they'd been installed to keep the women safe. The security men, who worked the day and night shifts, watched them, and if they got off on it, that was their business.

Faith saw to Mike, one of her regulars, nothing unusual going on. But perhaps it might soon, once Mike had gone. Faith would have the ideal opportunity to get to the money as Petra would need time to shift the clients around so Faith had more punters to attend to. The fact Faith had returned to work early had rung a massive alarm bell, and she could only be here for one thing.

The cash.

On the day Goldie had been killed, India had told him cash was taken every hour to the bank, but it had been a lie. She'd said it to see his reaction, to gauge whether he'd planned to rob her as well as the twins' casino. She had a high-tech safe, she wasn't bothered about anyone bursting in and stealing from her, but it seemed she had to be worried about Faith, who knew the code, nicking thousands of pounds for a scumbag called Austin Hunt.

India should inform George and Greg about him really, he lived on their estate, but she'd hold off until he'd taken the cash from the wheelie bin. One of the security men, Bungle (named after the bear in the old children's programme, *Rainbow*), had seen Austin digging into the bins on several occasions. India hadn't needed to put the feelers out to find out who he was because Satin had already informed her about the imminent theft as soon as she'd set him up to steal.

Satin, India's secret right-hand, always looked out for ways to give her something extra to do.

She knew of her deep-seated grief, how she needed an extra outlet to maim and kill. Satin engineered things to create issues, to trap people into doing something they shouldn't so they'd be caught red-handed. Cruel, perhaps, but India didn't give a shit about that. She *needed* the kills in order to remain sane.

People wove the most disastrous of webs, and she was the giant spider, waiting to pounce. Years ago, she would have looked before she leaped, rounding Austin and Faith up as soon as Satin had spilled the beans, *before* they had a chance to steal, but these days, with a decade of running an estate under her belt, she found it more satisfying to watch things unfold, *then* ensnare those who thought they could cross her.

She was sick in the head, she didn't need a therapist to tell her that, but her heart had been ravaged by Errol's death, her soul blackened so much it had ended up charred beyond recognition, and the pit inside her, fathoms deep and so achingly awful, needed to be filled with something.

A message tinkled on the burner, and she picked it up.

SATIN: AUSTIN JUST GOT HOLD OF ME. HE SENT HER TO WORK TODAY.

INDIA: I THOUGHT AS MUCH. WHAT'S THE SCORE?

SATIN: HE'S TOLD ME TO STOP HER ACCESSING THE SAFE.

INDIA: WHY?

SATIN: HE'S GOT OTHER MEANS OF GETTING THE MONEY.

INDIA: SUCH A SHAME. I WAS GOING TO HAVE FUN WITH HIM.

SATIN: YOU STILL COULD. HE PLANNED TO STEAL. JUST BECAUSE HE CALLED IT OFF, DOESN'T MEAN HE SHOULDN'T BE PUNISHED.

INDIA: TRUE. HAS HE CONTACTED FAITH YET?

SATIN: HE ASKED ME TO TELL HER.

INDIA: DON'T SAY A WORD. LET HER CONTINUE. DO WHAT YOU HAVE TO DO, JUST IN CASE SHE MAKES HER MOVE TODAY.

India got up and poured another coffee. Stared at the bricks on the other side of the alley. Smiled at the thought of taking Faith to the abattoir.

She'd soon be squealing like a stuck pig.

Chapter Eight

*T*he ride in the police car wasn't as exciting as
Faith had imagined. It wasn't a proper car with
flashing lights and the word POLICE on the side, it was
normal. Black. Bassett had said it would be better if
they didn't turn up in a panda. The less the neighbours
saw the better. Sergeant Smith hadn't gone with them.
Instead, another detective in a suit, Hamilton, had got
in the passenger seat.

"We're in my car because I want it to look like you didn't inform on him," Bassett said as he drove along. "You mentioned his friends, their families. Better that they think your husband grassed."

"He might well do," Mum said in the back next to Faith. "He'll probably say he left the man alive and his mates murdered him. Anything to get himself out of the shit."

Bassett turned into their street. "Would you like Faith to stay in the car?"

"No, he'll think something's up if she doesn't come in. Besides, he won't hit me in front of her."

"Well, we'll park a couple of doors down on the other side of the street, then get out once you've gone inside. I have to tell you, I'm not comfortable with this. Putting you in danger."

"I don't care. I'm collecting some of our things and that's final."

Bassett parked and sighed. "Leave the front door ajar if you can."

Mum got out and walked around the other side to collect Faith who trembled. A part of her wanted to tell Dad what was going to happen, that coppers were going to go inside and get him, but another part warned her to keep quiet. Murder was wrong, and if

Dad had killed that man, he should go to prison, shouldn't he?

Mum slid her key in the lock and twisted it. She pushed the door open and put one step over the threshold, then stopped. Looked up.

Faith did the same.

Dad hung from a thick rope over the banisters, his face purple and bloated, his mouth coated in froth. Stains dampened the fabric of his grey trousers, below the zip and between his legs. Faith stared, unable to comprehend what had happened, then fear kicked in, and she rushed to the detectives' car. In her panic, she struggled to open the driver's door. Bassett did it for her, taking her wrist and drawing her towards him.

"What's happened?"

"My dad, he's hanging…"

"Shit. Shit! Get in the back and stay there."

Faith managed to open the rear door and clambered inside. Bassett and Hamilton shot out and across the street to Mum who still stood with one foot in the doorway. Hamilton moved her out of the way, and Bassett rushed inside. Hamilton guided Mum over the road and helped her into the back seat.

Mum grabbed Faith and squeezed her tight. "Oh God, I wish you hadn't seen that."

But she had, and she'd never forget it. Never in a million years.

Clinton tucked Faith into one of the single beds in the back room of their house, Mum still down in the kitchen with Sally. He sat on the edge and read her a story, although he didn't hold a book. He spoke of turquoise seas and sunny skies again, of laughter and family, and told tales of the Jumbees, restless spirits, all the things his mother missed.

"Why doesn't she go home, then?" Faith asked, sleepy despite wanting to be on her guard. She didn't trust Clinton. All black people were bad.

"Here is home for her now."

"Does she miss St Thomas?"

"Oh yes."

"If it's so pretty and warm, why would she want to live here when she can live there? I'd want to stay there, I would."

"Life isn't as simple as that. Are you tired enough to sleep now?"

"Yeah."

He left the room, the door open a little, a slither of light from the landing slicing into the darkness. The stairs creaked with him going down them, and Faith closed her eyes, trying to imagine the St Thomas sea, but all that filled her mind was Dad hanging from the banisters.

Was he dead? She didn't know, no one had said, and while it had been nice of Clinton to tell her all about the Caribbean, she'd rather be told what was going on. Not knowing for sure scared her. Maybe her brain had filled in the blanks and he wasn't dead. Maybe Bassett had gone inside and cut him down. An ambulance had come before Hamilton had driven them to Sally's, but no one had brought her father out. Neighbours had congregated, though, many front doors open, the silhouettes of people standing on their steps giving the impression they were monsters. Dark monsters that fed on gossip.

She drifted, finally floating on the turquoise sea in a boat. Above, a dragon soared, but instead of being the kind creature in the book at the police station, it zoomed towards her, breathing fire, burning all the skin off her face.

She sat upright, breathing heavily, to the sound of Mum crying downstairs.

Would life ever go back to normal?

Chapter Nine

At the empty hairdresser's in the back room, George nodded. Anyone coming in here would think it was just a panelled wall, the paint nice and white. They'd be bloody wrong. A keypad on the other side of the room opened it. Behind the wooden panels in the centre, a steel sheet could be slid across, and behind that, deep shelving either side of a short corridor with several safes, guns, and the drugs they'd been buying cheap from the Sparrow Lot's suppliers. Moon had given them the blueprint for the hideaway, one he'd recently had installed in his bomb shelter. George, pleased with how it had turned out, reckoned they'd chosen the right place to store their stash.

It would be a legitimate working salon—they had to have *some* going concerns to explain why they had so much wealth, the taxman might come knocking otherwise—and they'd already employed all of their new stylists. Previous to being in the Noodle and Tiger, George hadn't found anyone suitable to be the one to let their men in to collect guns, he hadn't got the right vibe from the stylists they'd chosen, but chatting to Anna had solved that. She could do with the job, and her being a single mother had pulled at his heartstrings.

Would his need to look after women with children, abandoned by their men, ever leave him? It was tied to their mother, that desire to make sure the mums and kids didn't suffer, but with hundreds of people in the same situation on their estate...he couldn't help them all. He'd satisfied it by helping those who'd wandered across their path, telling himself Mum had sent them their way, convincing him there was a Heaven and she watched from there.

If he thought that, it meant she wasn't really gone. It meant he could cope with her loss. Vic, their therapist, had helped them both in that regard, and at least they now allowed themselves to mourn, which was something they'd never wanted to do before.

Who wanted to put themselves through pain?

But to be in pain meant they lived, they cared.

He cleared his throat. "Fuck it, let's open for business tomorrow."

"It was meant to be in two weeks," Greg said from the desk. "Why the change of plan?"

"The hairdressers need an income."

"But you already paid them a retainer."

"For Pete's sake, stop putting up roadblocks. We'll do what's called a soft opening, give a few free haircuts to those who can't afford it. I'll get what's-his-face to make up some posters. We'll stick them in the window. If they can prove they're on benefits, they get a new barnet."

"The girls might not be able to cope. There'll be loads of people coming in."

"All right, the first fifty people. With five hairdressers, that's ten customers each. Anyway, what do you think of this?" George gestured to the compartment.

"Pretty fucking nifty." Greg came to stand beside him. "A whole armoury and no one's any the wiser."

"Apart from Anna and our blokes."

Greg tutted. "That goes without saying. You're such a twat sometimes."

"Yeah, well, you should be used to it by now. I don't get why you have to comment on it when it's a given."

"I like reminding you."

"Gimp." George walked over to the keypad and prodded in the code to close the steel sheet then the wall. "What I don't like is you have to come all the way over here to shut it. Say we had a raid. What if Anna's not close enough to get it sorted before the pigs come in? Our blokes won't know the code for the keypad."

"There's a couple of remote controls, divvo."

George shoved his hands in his pockets. "I knew that."

"Don't lie. You forgot."

"Sod off."

"Forgetting isn't good." Greg turned from the wall and glared at him.

"I've had a lot on my mind."

"So have I, but I remembered."

"All right, you know-it-all. We can't all be perfect like you."

"I don't need you to be perfect, fuck knows you're not. What I need is for you to be on the ball. Mistakes happen. We don't want that going on here."

"Shut up now, you're getting on my nellies." George pulled a small packet of Tangtastics out of his pocket and opened them. "Want a sweet?"

"No, ta."

"Good, means more for me."

George got on with contacting Anna to ask her to get her arse into work tomorrow, plus he alerted the other girls and explained the free-haircut deal. Everyone responded positively, and he got a sense of excitement from them. All of them had been on the dole, eking out an existence, and they'd swooped in and changed all that.

Kings of the East End, we are.

He went through tonight in his head. They'd have to come here and collect the drugs to take to

Austin. Then they'd follow him to Mrs Whitehall's house to make sure he didn't stop along the way. Once he'd reported that he'd dropped the package off, they'd pay him.

If all went well, they might use Austin for other things.

This doing good lark was addictive.

Chapter Ten

Austin's heart rate hadn't calmed down since he'd texted Satin. What if Faith still went ahead? What if she got caught and told Mrs Whitehall it had been his idea? He'd lose his new job with The Brothers—there was no way he could let Faith carry on, not now he had a weekly drop at the leader's house. He'd only got hold of

Satin because Faith hadn't been answering him. He supposed she'd be working with a client.

He stared at the message string.

AUSTIN: GET HOLD OF FAITH TO CANCEL THE PLANS. I DON'T NEED THE MONEY NOW. GOT ANOTHER WAY TO GET CASH.

SATIN: BUT WHAT ABOUT THE CUT YOU PROMISED ME? FUCKING HELL, YOU CAN'T JUST BAIL LIKE THAT!

AUSTIN: I NEVER WANTED TO NICK ANYTHING IN THE FIRST PLACE, BUT I WAS DESPERATE. IT WAS YOU WHO TOLD ME ABOUT THE MONEY ANYWAY. IF YOU NEED IT SO MUCH, SPLIT IT WITH FAITH OR STEAL IT YOURSELF.

SATIN: I DON'T KNOW THE SAFE CODE. GOD, YOU'RE SUCH A LOSER.

Why couldn't anything go right for once? His life was a complete fuck-up, all his own doing. If only he hadn't treated Maxine badly, none of this would be happening. Vic had told him he had to concentrate on accepting the blame, admitting he'd been the one to bring everything crashing down. To embrace the truth meant he could move on, but it wasn't working. Yes, he knew he'd been a dick, but nothing had got better.

All right, The Brothers had come and offered him that job, but what if it really was a trick? What if Faith *had* grassed him up?

Not knowing sent him straight to the cupboard. He poured himself a small shot of whisky and downed it. It'd be out of his system by the time he did the drug run. The urge to pour more came over him, and he fought it. He thought of something Vic had said.

"If temptation isn't standing before you, you won't be drawn in."

Austin tipped all of his alcohol down the sink, every single bottle. Having it hidden in the cupboard was still a tease because he knew it was there. Drink had played a big part in getting into this mess, and he couldn't be doing with continuing down that path. Pleased with himself, he dumped the bottles outside the back door—he'd take them to the recycle bank when he went out later—then locked up and went for the kettle. Extra amounts of coffee would have to be his new vice.

The doorbell rang, and he sidled down the hallway, his back to the wall, anxious about who'd come calling. Could it be the twins again? They hadn't given him any details about tonight, like what time he had to leave, so he had no idea about the state of play. Maybe they'd come back with instructions and his five hundred quid.

Something told him to check before he opened the door. He nipped into the living room and peered out of the window.

Oh shit. What was *he* doing here?

Benny Bender stood on the doorstep, alone. His two-tone suit, in shades of grey and turquoise, reminded Austin of the mods years ago. The quiff hairdo, held fast with wet-look gel, gave him an old-fashioned vibe, or maybe it was coming back into fashion again. Austin didn't have the foggiest.

He checked the street. Benny's car over the road with one of the heavies in the driver's seat. Shit and bollocks.

The bell rang again, followed by Benny knocking with the side of his fist. "Open up, you fucking little twat!"

Austin swallowed his fear and went to the door, opening it with a shaky hand. "All right, Benny?"

"Took you long enough. What were you doing?"

"Been cleaning."

"You bastard fanny." Benny brushed past and strode into the kitchen.

Austin shut the door and went after him. "Want a coffee? I was just about to have one."

Benny leaned against the larder door. "What were the twins doing here?"

Austin closed his eyes momentarily. He was being watched. But this could go in his favour. He stared at Benny. "They asked me to do a job for them."

"So you didn't get hold of them to pay protection money? Against me?"

"What?" Austin half laughed. "Err, why would I do that?"

"Because I'm putting pressure on you to pay more than we agreed."

"I'll be able to pay you off pretty quickly now."

Benny seemed ultra-interested. "Is that right? What job is it?"

"I dunno, they haven't told me yet, just said they wanted me to do something."

"Convenient."

"What d'you mean?"

"Well, you not knowing what they want you to do."

"It's true, I haven't got a chuffing clue."

"When you know, tell me."

"What for?"

"Because I fucking *said* so." Benny glared at him. "Until you've paid me off, you belong to me, you got that?"

Austin reckoned he belonged to the twins now, but he didn't point that out. Benny was small fry compared to them.

Maybe I should have told them. Asked for my wages in lieu. Got Benny off my case now instead of later.

"Did you want a coffee, then?" Austin asked, going for casual.

"I don't drink instant." Benny turned his nose up. "When are you doing the job?"

"I don't know that either."

"You're lying to me. I don't like liars."

"Look, I swear, they came in, said they wanted me to do a job, then that was it. I didn't ask questions because it was them. I mean, who the fuck asks them shit? You just get on and do it, don't you, accept what they say."

"If I find out you've told me fibs, you won't be working for anyone again, do I make myself clear?"

"Yeah, of course."

Austin would like to think he wasn't frightened of Benny, that he could take him down in a fight if he had to, but he couldn't. His henchmen were nutters, and they shit him right up. Benny ruled his little empire with his blokes at his back, evil threats so people toed the line, and to upset him meant you got paid a visit.

Should I fuck this and just tell the twins about him?

Were they mates with Prince? Could they have a word on his behalf and ask him to get Benny to stop menacing people? It hadn't worked when Austin had tried it, but surely George and Greg would have more sway.

"I'll be on my way, then." Benny straightened his jacket fronts. "Remember, I want the extra five hundred by the end of the week."

How could I forget? "Will...will it go up anymore after that?"

Benny smiled. "It might well do, seeing as you're working for the twins now. I heard they pay well. What you never had you don't miss, so they say, so handing over the dosh they pay you won't be a problem, will it."

Austin couldn't help himself, couldn't hold it back. "Why did you go against the agreement?"

Benny laughed. "Why the fuck not?"

He breezed out, slamming the front door behind him.

Austin slapped his hands over his eyes and breathed deeply. What if Benny changed the goalposts again? What if he decided to add extra interest? With no contract in place, he could rinse Austin for as long as he wanted. What if this went on forever, Austin paying him a grand or more a month?

He dragged his hands down his face.

He was going to tell the twins.

Chapter Eleven

Faith had waved Mike off fifteen minutes ago. She'd showered and put on loungewear provided by Mrs Whitehall. It was now or never. She had to get in that little office and take the money. Rush downstairs to put it in the wheelie bin. Come back up, because by then, Petra would have sorted her clients for the rest of the day.

She left her room, taking a few deeps breaths in the corridor. As far as she was aware, the place didn't have cameras, but all the same, she sensed someone watching. Or was that her guilty conscience spying on her? She swallowed, her mouth dry, hands shaking, and crept down the corridor, past the other closed doors. At the end, she paused in front of Len's office. What if he or Vanda were in there?

She thought about it. No, Len wouldn't be in, not today. He did the books twice a week, so she'd only have Vanda to contend with. Still, Faith held the money Mike had paid her, so she had a legitimate reason for going into the office if anyone came along and caught her.

She twisted the handle.

Now was the time to turn back if she was going to.

She stepped inside.

No one sat at the desk, the computer screen dark, so none of the women had been in recently. That was the rule—the client left, the women handed the money over to Vanda or Faith, they added the details to the spreadsheet on the computer, then went back to work. Vanda, Faith, or Len put the money in the safe.

She closed the door. Procrastinated by logging on and adding Mike's visit to the sheet. She glanced at the safe where it stood on the floor, then back at the screen. If she didn't go through with this, she wouldn't be able to leave London as quickly as she wanted to, but without Lemon around to siphon her wages, she'd be able to save some. Another six months, and if she did extra shifts, she'd soon have what she needed. Could she stand to hold her dreams off for a while longer?

She logged out. Went over to the safe and crouched. Put in the code, expecting it to be wrong, that this was a setup and Austin had been playing with her all this time, maybe working for Mrs Whitehall to flush out those who couldn't be trusted. But the door unlocked, and she swung it open.

Thousands of pounds stared back at her. She added Mike's payment to a pile that wasn't inside elastic bands. She gripped her hair either side and wrenched. Could she live in her street if she didn't do this and he told her neighbours she was a slag? Would it matter what they thought?

Yes, it would. What she'd been through at fourteen had paved the way for her living with a deep sense of shame. The idea of people she saw every day, knowing what she was… She'd kept her teenage secret to herself for so long, thinking people would say she'd 'asked for it', and some of them were so nasty she didn't think they'd understand her working in the sex trade.

She had to remember she'd only been a child. It hadn't been her fault. And this job hadn't been her fault either. Reggie had forced her into selling her body, and she'd continued doing it, even after he'd fucked off.

Was she punishing herself for what had happened all those years ago? Did she think she wasn't worth anything except being a sex worker? Was allowing men to paw at her something she thought she deserved?

She snatched a money bag that had been folded to one side and stuffed the wads of cash into it. She took it all and shut the safe. Finding an elastic band in the desk drawer, she twisted the top of the bag and secured it, then stuffed it into her knickers. The bag had too much in it, so it bulged, and while she had baggy joggers on, it was still obvious she'd hidden something.

Shit. She had to walk through reception yet, where Petra was bound to notice, her and her eagle eyes.

Faith hadn't thought this through properly.

She grabbed the black bag out of the flip-top bin, put the money bag inside, and tied the top. Out in the corridor, she heaved in a big breath and marched down it. No one would bat an eye, she'd taken rubbish out the back before. In reception, she clocked punters waiting on the sofas but no Petra.

Desperate to get this over and done with, she legged it downstairs, walking through the storeroom where Shitty Sharon still unboxed the new stock. What was she, on a go-slow?

"Here's another belter." Shitty held up a turquoise lace thing. "Twenty quid with staff discount. That's going straight in my basket."

Faith forced a smile and pushed the outside door open, stomping towards the wheelie bins. A quick rip to the side of the black sack so Austin would know which one contained the money, and she slung it in a bin. Relieved her part was over, she returned inside and ignored Shitty who flapped a hand for her to come over and look at some whips.

"Too busy," Faith called.

Upstairs, still no Petra, Faith went into her room and locked the door. She took her phone out of her handbag and brought up the last text from Austin so she could reply.

Oh God, he'd called the theft off. Why hadn't she checked her phone before now? Fucking hell!

FAITH: IT'S DONE. LEFT-HAND BIN. BLACK BAG HAS A SPLIT IN IT. DROP MY CUT ROUND LATER, THEN FUCK OFF OUT OF MY LIFE.

Chapter Twelve

India had followed Faith's movements on CCTV. At one point, when Faith had grabbed at her hair, she'd thought she was going to bottle it. But no, greed had played a part—or perhaps it was her fear of Austin—and she'd snatched that money up as if her life had depended on it.

Silly woman.

It could be considered cruel, what India had allowed to happen. Austin had frightened Faith into doing what he wanted, his desperation forcing him to behave differently to how he usually would. All this, engineered so India could have a little fun. Yet it wasn't just that. Faith could have come to her the second Austin had approached her, but she hadn't. She could have proved her loyalty, but she hadn't. Instead, she'd gone along with it, and now look, all that money in a wheelie bin, just waiting for Austin to collect it.

India settled down to watch, her monitor showing the three angles pointed towards the bins. She'd let him take the cash, let him think he'd got away with it.

Then she'd strike.

Chapter Thirteen

*D*ad had indeed died, of course he had, and to honour him, Faith had remembered what he'd taught her. Despite seeing Clinton every day while they stayed with him and Sally, she kept her hatred hidden, pretending she wasn't a racist cow in front of him, Sally, or her mother.

Except she was. It had burrowed into her bones, and she didn't know how to get it out. Her vehement dislike *of black people had increased after Dad's death, steadily growing as time rolled by, because if they hadn't gone to Sally and Clinton's, Dad wouldn't have killed himself. If Mum hadn't threatened to tell on him, he wouldn't have been trapped down a blind alley with nowhere to run.*

Life without him had been easier, she could at least admit that. Mum was so much happier without the threat of a punch coming her way. It had all come out one night when Mum and Sally had sat up drinking wine. Faith had listened, sitting on the stairs. How Mum had suffered abuse, and Faith had felt sorry for her but at the same time asked herself what Mum had done to deserve it. If Faith had been naughty, Dad had smacked her. Mum must have been naughty, too, and that's why he'd given her a thump. She must have deserved it.

Was Faith wicked for thinking that way? For trying to convince herself that Dad had been good when he hadn't? She didn't want to face the truth, that much was obvious, so she romanticised the past so it fitted better with how she'd seen him. The alternative, acknowledging he'd had a dark side, hurt too much.

They hadn't been back to their little home since Dad had hanged himself. Mum couldn't stand to go there, so they'd kipped at Sally's. Clinton had told Faith more stories at bedtime about St Thomas, always with the door open, and while she didn't want to like him, he did tell a good tale. She saw it all in her head, what he described, and he promised to take everyone to Notting Hill Carnival next year so she could listen to the steel drums.

A bad person wouldn't do that, would they?

After the funeral, the neighbours rallied round, packing everything up and moving them into another place in the next street, Clinton borrowing a big van from work to ferry it there. He'd been nice to them, Faith couldn't deny that, and she hated him for being kind, for proving what Mum had said, that black people were the same as anyone else.

Why was life so confusing?

A year later, Tim came on the scene. A blind date, and Mum had fallen head over heels. In no time, he'd installed himself in their life and their house, and Faith had seethed, angry that Dad could be forgotten so easily, so quickly.

"Why's he staying here?" she asked an hour before Tim was due home from work.

117

A rich man, he had what seemed like endless amounts of money and had suggested they move yet again to a house he was thinking of buying. Mum wanted to stay where they were, amongst her friends, and so his suggestion had been put to bed. At least he'd listened. He hadn't forced the issue like Dad would have.

Faith didn't know what Tim did, but every morning he put on snazzy suits and shiny leather shoes that Mum said cost a fortune, more than a month's rent. His dark hair, slicked back, always had perfect comb lines in it, and he trimmed his moustache once a week, leaving the hairs in the sink. Mum didn't mind, which was odd, because she'd shouted at Dad if he'd shaved and left a mess.

"I deserve happiness," Mum said. "Those years with your dad... You'll understand one day." She stirred some posh sauce or other. Lately, Mum had been cooking fancy meals.

Faith wanted to understand now. "Why did he hit you?"

"We're not talking about that, not today."

"But —"

Mum slapped the wooden spoon on the worktop, sauce splashing on the nearby kettle and her new cream blouse. "I don't want to think about him. He did bad things, not just to me, and we're well shot of him. Now lay the table."

Faith got on with it, sulking. Mum must know she'd heard everything at the police station, but she hadn't spoken about that either. Once again, Faith tried to imagine Dad stamping on someone's head, walking away, not caring whether he was dead or not. Mum going with him, too scared to open her mouth. It was so different to how she'd been in the months before his death that Faith struggled to envisage her mother being meek and mild back then.

On one of their wine nights, Sally had said, "He was a coward. Couldn't even take the rap for what he'd done. Killed his damn self before the police got to him. You did the right thing, so don't go blaming yourself."

Faith put a fork down beside a placemat. If she'd been Mum, she'd have kept Dad's secret forever.

She'd tried to hate Tim, but he was too nice. He bought her clothes and pretty shoes, sweets, dolls, whatever she wanted, but never had he hugged her like Dad had, saying people might think he was a pervert. At the time, aged eleven, Faith hadn't understood what he'd meant, until she'd reached fourteen and he had hugged her. And touched her where he shouldn't, his hand on her backside.

Mum hadn't seemed to notice.

She woke suddenly. Something was wrong, but she didn't know what. She blinked, her heart thundering at the sight of the black figure crouching beside the bed.

"This is our little secret," he said, stroking her leg.

Faith panicked and glanced around her bedroom. Where was Mum? What time was it?

She looked towards the window. No sunlight nudged through the gap in the curtains, only blackness filling the slice. The house, so silent save for his ragged breathing, seemed to wait for her to scream. She wanted to, but no matter how hard she tried, nothing came out. Her voice, locked away inside her, bubbled for release, and she willed herself to make some noise.

"It's time. I've been patient enough. Now, you're going to be a good girl and let me do whatever I want."

Her chest hurt from where she held her breath, so she let it out in a big rush, her face getting hot. Tears stung, and she bit her bottom lip.

His hand moved higher.

When had he taken the quilt off? How long had he been in here while she'd slept?

"If you tell anyone, something bad will happen to your mum."

Finally, she screamed, although it was pitiful, more of a whimper.

He laughed, his shadow looming closer, his breath warm on her bare arm. "She won't hear you. That wine she drank before bed…I put something in it."

The next morning, Faith didn't want to go downstairs. Or to school. Or even be here. Had Dad felt like this, so trapped? She imagined getting some rope and putting it around her neck like he had, but… She didn't have the courage to face the pain of suffocating or the snap of her neck.

Tim had gone already, his engine loud compared to other people's, what with him having a posh sports car with a double exhaust, so she forced herself to go into the bathroom and have a shower, something Tim had paid someone to fit. She scrubbed between her legs, then her whole body, scratching her skin to get the top layer off, the layer he'd touched. Red raw, she got out and dried her sore body, then brushed her teeth over and over, because he'd been in her mouth, too.

Back in the bedroom, she dressed, the fabric of her clothes scratchy, and she let the tears fall. He'd done things no man should do to a child, and a part of her wanted to keep it to herself. A sense of shame filled her, so great she went hot all over, and she sat on the edge of the bed. Glanced across.

Blood stained the bottom sheet.

She ripped the bedding off and bundled it up, anger taking the place of humiliation and the intense emotion of disgust. She rushed downstairs, her face wet with tears, and flew into the kitchen.

Mum turned from the sink and smiled. "Tim's bought you a lovely present. It's on the table there, look."

Faith clutched the bedding to her and stared at the velvet box on her placemat. All those things he'd bought her before, they'd been leading to…this. Bribes. "I don't want anything from him.*"*

"Oh, not this again. Pack it in, all right? I know, I know, he's not your dad, but for fuck's sake, Tim's a damn sight better than he ever was, so just accept we're together. Listen, I'm really tired, think I'm coming down with something, so I don't want any of your lip."

"Would Dad have raped me?"

Mum gaped. "Excuse me?"

"You heard." Faith threw the sheets towards her. "There's blood on there. Ask him what he was doing in my room last night."

Mum blinked. "What? I mean…what?"

"He didn't put a condom on so…"

"Oh, Jesus Christ." Mum staggered to a chair and sank onto it. "Tim? You're saying Tim raped you?"

A sob hijacked Faith's answer. Why wasn't Mum giving her a cuddle? Why had she asked that question instead of believing her?

"Are you sure you weren't dreaming?"

Faith stared at her, uncomprehending. "I hate you and I don't care if something bad happens to you, not now."

"What does that mean?"

"Ask Tim!"

Faith ran from the house, scarpering down the street, blinded by tears. She kept going until she reached the police station, desperate for someone to listen to her. Had she made a mistake by having a shower?

A uniformed officer looked up from behind the reception desk. "Are you okay?"

She shook her head. "I've been raped."

Words she'd never thought she'd say.

Chapter Fourteen

Austin's legs almost gave out from under him. What? Faith had stolen the money? Why hadn't Satin passed on his message? Why hadn't Faith seen the ones he'd sent? Or had she, and she'd decided to go along with it anyway? He read the message again, just to make sure.

FAITH: IT'S DONE. LEFT-HAND BIN. BLACK BAG HAS A SPLIT IN IT. DROP MY CUT ROUND LATER, THEN FUCK OFF OUT OF MY LIFE.

He should leave it there. Have nothing to do with it. Satin's plan had been stupid anyway, too much of a risk, and only his desperation had thought it was a good idea to proceed. If he stopped using his unregistered SIM and got a new one, no one could pin the theft on him because he could claim that wasn't his number. He'd say he didn't know what Satin or Faith were on about.

But that was a lot of cash…

Don't be greedy. Leave the money where it is. You can pay Benny off in about two months. Just a few weeks, and this will all be over.

Then he remembered what Benny had said, that he might change the rules again. Wasn't it better to pay him off in a lump now, get something down on paper that said he owed nothing, then move on? Maybe get out of London? If Benny and his lot didn't know where he lived, they couldn't come and torment him.

But they'll find me anyway.

Sod this. He'd go and see the twins now. Confess everything. He'd rather face them than Mrs Whitehall, who was rumoured to be worse.

But that money's just sitting there…

He stared his future in the eye, where he was caught taking the bag out of the bin, Mrs Whitehall's men dragging him into the sex shop and beating the shit out of him.

FML.

He grabbed his keys and left the house. Got in the car and drove to The Whitehall Estate, all the while trying to talk himself out of it. He parked in front of a row boutique shops off High Street, paid for the ticket using cash. A quick glance around, checking for any traps, anyone watching, and he was off down the delivery access alley. At the newly painted green gate, he twisted the metal loop handle and entered the yard. No one around. He legged it over to the left-hand bin and opened the lid.

Just like she'd said, a black sack with a rip in it. He tore it further, revealing a fabric money bag near the top on a bed of scrunched-up paper and empty takeaway Costa cups, an elastic band keeping it closed. Snatching it out, he peered up at the building—no one stared down from the windows.

Not wanting to linger, he'd be a dick if he did, he ran out of the yard and back to his car.

Shaking, he flung the bag on the passenger seat, hoping it actually contained money and it wasn't a trick, because if he got caught down the line for a bag stuffed with Monopoly notes or something, it would all have been for nothing.

He'd die for nothing.

He drove off, his heart thundering, his arms and legs shaking. At a housing estate, he stopped outside a high-rise and reached across for the money bag. Tugged at the elastic band so hard it broke, the end whipping round and snapping at his finger.

He stared at the contents.

"Jesus Christ…"

He took it out and counted one of the stacks — a thousand pounds. He totted up how many stacks there were, and if they were all a grand, he had thirty here. Enough for Benny, Satin's and Faith's cuts, and some left over for himself.

Despite the fear, he laughed. Then he gunned the engine and drove to The Judas Estate, his worries abating the farther he went. It would be all right, wouldn't it? He could do what he'd thought and ditch his SIM once he'd seen Benny. Satin had said the yard had no cameras, and she must be telling the truth, otherwise he'd have been caught snooping in the bins way before now.

He was home and dry, right?

He came to a halt outside the Goose and Gander where Benny conducted meetings with his customers. The lender's car was here. Austin sorted ten grand—more than he owed Benny now, but the extra would show goodwill—then stashed the rest in the glove box. He took his phone out.

AUSTIN: I'VE GOT ALL OF YOUR CASH. I'M OUTSIDE.

BENNY: WON THE LOTTERY, HAVE YOU?

AUSTIN: NO, I GOT ANOTHER LOAN OFF SOMEONE ELSE.

He got out of the car, leaving the ten grand on the passenger seat under one of his hoodies. He wanted assurance first that this was the end. Benny strutted out of the pub on his own. Austin wasn't stupid—his men would be inside, watching.

"Quite the entrepreneur, aren't you?" Benny said.

"I want this over. I need you to tell me this is it, that when I hand over the money, we're done."

"But what if I don't want to be done?"

"Then I'll go to The Brothers for protection."

Benny appeared unfazed bar a slight tic beside one eye. "Fair enough. I was getting bored fucking about with you anyway. How much have you got?"

"Ten grand."

"That'll do nicely. Give it over, then."

"Send me a text first, saying you won't be coming for more."

Benny sighed. "If my solicitor was here, I'd even get him to type you an official letter, but he isn't. Jesus." He tapped in a text.

So long as Austin had a record of the message, he had proof. His phone beeped, and he read the text. Not trusting Benny, he got back in the car. Locked himself in. Grabbed the money and opened the window just enough to hand it over.

Benny took it, eyebrows hiking up. "I'll have to count it, obviously."

"Fine, but we're finished now."

Austin sped away, slowing at the car park entrance. He looked in the rearview mirror. Benny stood where he'd left him, the wads of cash in his hands.

"Fuck you, arsehole."

Austin drove to The Cardigan Estate.

In The Angel, the old SIM in a cheapo burner, a new one in his proper phone, he waited for Lisa, the manager, to contact the twins for him. He had to give them his new number anyway, assuming they'd still want him to deliver the drugs after his confession. He needed them on his side. He'd contemplated them seeing it from his point of view and agreeing they'd look after him, but he'd also envisaged what would happen if they didn't take kindly to him nicking off another leader. They might march him straight to Mrs Whitehall for punishment.

He drank some of his Coke and waited for his grub to arrive, although he might be too nervous to eat. But he needed food—who knew, if the twins decided to take him somewhere for a beating, hold him hostage, he might not get anything for a while.

A slender young man brought his meal and cutlery, and Austin tucked in. Minced beef pie, mash, mushy peas, and gravy. It reminded him of Maxine's cooking, and a lump of emotion swelled in his throat. He swallowed tightly, wishing he could turn back the clock and go to a time where he could actually fix things. His behaviour with Maxine, all that stuff. But he couldn't, he was stuck in this mess, and he'd have to do what Vic had told him and face what he'd done, own it, and accept the consequences.

He seemed to wade through his food, every mouthful a penance, and once the lad had come back to take his plate, Austin got up to buy another Coke.

Lisa served him.

"Are they coming?" he asked.

"Yep, they won't be long."

He took his drink to his seat and sipped, one eye on the door. A couple of minutes later, the twins walked in, George in the lead, and they headed straight for Austin. His guts cramped—fuck, was he going to shit himself?—and he wanted to bolt.

No. Tell them everything.

George plonked down in the chair beside him, Greg taking a pew opposite.

"I think this needs to be in private," Greg said. "We've had a report that you paid a visit to Mrs Whitehall's yard."

Austin's bowels contracted. They'd had him tailed? "Um, yeah?"

George jerked his head and stood. "Come with us."

Austin left his Coke and followed them through the double doors into the area where the toilets were. George opened another door and led the way down a corridor. At yet another door, he pressed a bell button, looked up at a camera, and gave the thumbs-up. The door buzzed open, and George strode through. Austin had never been back here, although he'd heard what went on. They stood in what appeared to be a reception area.

George said to an older redheaded woman behind the desk, "We'll be in here for a bit."

"Do you want any drinks?"

"Nah."

George went into a room, waiting for Greg and Austin to file in. Greg sat on a sofa, and George gestured for Austin to sit opposite.

George closed the door and leaned on it. "What's going on?"

"You're going to hate me…"

"Maybe, but spill the beans before I get arsey. I don't like people wasting our time."

Austin launched into his abridged tale, watching The Brothers every so often to gauge their reactions. Neither of them showed anything in their expressions. It was as if they were carved out of marble they were that stiff. He hadn't mentioned Faith yet. Maybe he could keep her out of it. All he'd said was he needed money, he'd borrowed off Benny, then Satin had told him about the safe. But if he didn't mention Faith and they already knew everything from her, he'd be caught out lying...

Fucking hell.

"So, um, can you help me?" His heart rate had done a number on him throughout the story, and he reckoned he'd be sick if they didn't answer him soon.

Greg shifted forward to sit on the edge of the sofa. He widened his legs, stuck his elbows on his knees, and let his hands drape between them. "Sounds like you got yourself into a bit of a pickle."

"I was a mess. Maxine leaving, it fucked me over. I didn't know if I was coming or going."

"So you decided it was a good idea to nick off Mrs Whitehall."

Austin sighed. "I didn't think of that, I told you, Satin suggested it."

"Yet you went ahead anyway," George said. "I'm a bit disappointed if I'm honest. I mean, I wanted to help you, hence the drug-drop job. I sent you to Vic because I *knew* you needed help. I asked you if there was anything you wanted to tell us about why you needed money — if I recall, you said you had a monkey on your back. Why didn't you say the monkey was Benny Bender?"

"Because he kept sending his men round. I agreed to an amount I'd pay him back each month, yeah, and he said that was fine. I paid him, thought everything was all right, then two blokes turned up at my house, saying Benny wanted another five hundred. I didn't have it, I've got child support to pay, but they wanted it by the end of this week. Then they came again, saying if I didn't pay, there'd be consequences. *Then*, just this morning, *Benny* showed up at my gaff. It's all intimidation tactics, know what I mean? I reckon they go round shitting loads of people up for a laugh."

"Probably, and it's none of our concern — unless he's coming here and doing it, which he has." George glanced at Greg. "We can have him for that. Prince won't be able to say a thing about it because it's happening on our estate."

"I went to see him, Prince," Austin said and explained what had gone on. "He doesn't want to know."

Greg scowled. "So you're saying he's aware Benny and his men have been threatening you, *here*, on Cardigan?"

"Yeah, he said Benny's a legitimate lender so…"

George raised his eyebrows at his brother. "Seems we need to pay Prince a little visit to remind him how things work."

Relief poured into Austin. They were prepared to help. But what if that was only because Prince and Benny had broken the rules? They might have other ideas for Austin.

"There's more," he said.

"Oh, fuck me…" George pushed off the door and paced. "Go on."

"Satin told me to rope Faith into it."

George stopped, mouth hanging open. "Faith Lemon?"

"Yeah, she said I had to threaten Faith, get her to nick the money because she's one of four who know the safe code. I texted her earlier to call it off, but Faith messaged to say the cash was in the wheelie bin. I went to collect it, then gave ten grand to Benny."

"Right. Where's the rest?"

"In my glove box."

"Fuck me sideways… Anyone could nick that! Go and get it. I'll come with you."

Austin followed George out through the fire exit. Austin couldn't get his bearings, and he glanced around. The graveyard lay ahead, so he went left, then left again where a few cars, including the twins' BMW, had been parked next to the pub. He jogged across the street to his car, pulled the money bag out, then returned to George who waited beside some steel steps.

He handed the cash over. "That's Satin's and Faith's cut plus a bit left over. I don't want anything to do with it."

"At least you're prepared to forgo any extra in your pocket."

Austin couldn't work out if that was sarcastic or not.

Back in the room, he sat, his nerves bunched as George inspected the money.

The big man laughed, his head thrown back, and once he'd composed himself, he wiped at his eyes. "Fucking Nora. You couldn't make this up if you tried. I think Mrs Whitehall was already onto you, mate."

Austin frowned. "What do you mean?"

"The cash is fake."

The bottom dropped out of Austin's world. "*What?*"

"It's counterfeit. You just handed Benny Bender ten grand he can't spend." George gave him the bag back. "Get rid of it, all right?"

Austin's phone chirped, and he fished the cheap burner out of his pocket. Stared at the screen. "Oh fuck, he's got hold of me."

George laughed again. "I expect he's just made a similar discovery to me. Jesus Christ, this is funny."

Austin wasn't laughing.

BENNY: YOU TRIED TO STIFF ME, YOU CUNT. I'M GUNNING FOR YOU NOW. TEN GRAND IN FAKE NOTES? THINK I WOULDN'T NOTICE? KEEP ONE EYE OPEN WHEN YOU SLEEP, YOU BASTARD!

Austin trembled, and his food threatened to come up. He held the phone out for George to see what had been said.

"Oh dear. Looks like you've got yourself in hot water." He thumbed in a reply. A message

138

beeped back, and George passed the phone across.

AUSTIN: BRING IT ON, FUCKER! MEET ME AT THE NAKED FOUNTAIN ON CARDIGAN AT SEVEN O'CLOCK.

BENNY: WHO THE HELL ARE YOU CALLING FUCKER? AND YOU'D BETTER HAVE REAL CASH THIS TIME…

Austin's arsehole clenched. "What…what did you say *that* for?"

"Because, God forgive us, we're going to help you, and in order to do that, we need to pick the wanker up."

"Why are we helping?" Greg asked.

"Because I think we've just stumbled into one of Mrs Whitehall's little games."

Greg shook his head. "Shit. She's a cruel cow sometimes."

Confused, Austin stared from one twin to the other. "Games?"

George nodded. "Hmm. That's another story, though. We've got more important things to deal with. When we meet Benny, you'll be bait."

"B-bait?"

George looked down at him, his stare admonishing. "You have to work for your supper, sunshine. Nothing comes for free in *our* game."

Chapter Fifteen

India had watched the yard footage several times, enjoying it more with every viewing. Had Austin discovered the money was fake yet? Had he tried to spend some, and the shop had refused to take the cash? Or had he gone to the bank to deposit it, to launder it, and they'd spotted it was counterfeit?

She wished she'd been a fly on the wall since he'd left the yard.

The door knocked, and she asked, "Who is it?"

"Satin with your food, boss."

A ruse. She'd sent Satin down the road to the Belgian pâtisserie for a celebratory waffle, something they indulged in while setting people up, and afterwards, to celebrate their success. Also, it would stop Faith wondering whether Satin had come in here to grass on her. Not that she'd see Satin coming into the office anyway—she entertained a client at the moment, her antics on full display on the monitor.

"Come in."

Satin entered carrying a white box and posh coffees in a holder. She closed the door, locking it, as was the custom when they talked about things of this nature. No one would have the guts to barge in, but you couldn't be too sure, could you.

"Pop them on the coffee table," India said, "and get some plates and dessert forks out of the sideboard."

Satin did that, and India got up from behind her desk and perched on her recliner. She took a chocolate-drenched waffle out of the box and put it on a plate, her mouth watering at the variety of nuts sprinkled on top. Satin took her treat out — white chocolate with stripes of raspberry sauce and crushed Flake — and they both ate, India savouring the taste of something so naughty. They didn't need to speak, not yet. Each of them enjoyed playing these games, they were both as wicked as each other, and their ritual of indulging in something from the bakery while in the midst of a setup was the best part.

Waffles finished, they started on the coffee, sipping thoughtfully, the orchestrated intermission in the play exactly the same as all the others. Silent. Calm. Brilliant.

Finally, after the last sip, India placed her cup down. "I propose leaving them for a day or two, letting them think they've got away with it. I want Austin to drop Faith's cut to her — I need eyes in place to see her taking it. Photos, the usual drill."

She thought of Errol and how he'd be disappointed in her for doing this, trapping people for fun. She pushed it away. He was no longer here, and she had to do *something* to assuage the gnawing grief inside her.

"I'll get Bungle on it, shall I?" Satin asked.

"Yes, he's the less conspicuous of the two. The photos will serve to prove to Faith that she's lying when she tells me she doesn't know what I'm talking about at the confrontation."

"She won't like the abattoir."

India smiled. "Not many people do, as we've witnessed. Cassie Grafton's father from up north gave me that idea, the abattoir. He's dead now, but as you know, Cassie took over, although she's swanned off somewhere, leaving Jimmy to hold the reins."

"She's the one with the meat factory on the Barrington Patch." Satin smirked. "You said what goes on there."

"Hmm. The machine called Marlene, used specifically to mince people."

Satin laughed, her eyes scrunched shut. "Oh God, you should buy one."

"I'm one step ahead of you there. Ours arrived last week." India imagined feeding Faith—minus her teeth—into the large tunnel at the top then watching her minced body coming out of a chute on the side. "Faith messed with the wrong person."

Satin composed herself. "She didn't technically mess, though. *We* messed with *her*."

"Same thing."

They cracked up, India's blood coursing with the heat of retribution. "I do like these little schemes of yours that show the employees up for who they really are. Any news yet on whether Sharon's stolen those two pieces of lingerie she's been admiring this morning?"

"Sadly, she paid for them about an hour ago."

"Oh bugger. I'd hoped we could add her to our rota. Still, I should be glad she's loyal and wouldn't steal from me."

She switched her mind away from Sharon. She'd feed Faith's and Austin's mince to her dogs, perhaps commission her jeweller to make something pretty out of their teeth. Make them look like small pearls. She could drape a necklace around her throat, or perhaps a bracelet would be nicer.

Something to look forward to.

"What's happened to you?" Errol's voice, or her conscience, she wasn't sure which. *"You know what I feel about persecution."*

She did. His parents had been treated abysmally by the so-called lovely English, and here she was, using people as though they were commodities, something she owned and could do whatever she wanted with.

If you hadn't died, I wouldn't be doing this... I wouldn't feel so broken.

She glanced at her phone and frowned. The twins were calling, perhaps about the drop-off tonight. "Business," she said.

Satin made to rise. "Do you want me to leave?"

"Don't be silly. I'll put it on speaker." India accepted the call. "Good afternoon, boys. What can I do for you on this glorious day?"

"Glorious because you've been fucking about with two of our residents?"

"Oh, you don't sound happy." India smiled at Satin. "But the rules have been adhered to. They've done something on *my* estate so—"

"Debatable if they've been set up. You've openly admitted you do shit for sport."

"Oh, I assure you, Satin approached Austin in my shop on *my* turf. If he went to Faith on *your* estate, then your quibble is with him, not me."

"Why did you pick those two?"

"Why not? Satin saw an opportunity and took it. Now, if you've quite finished poking your nose into my affairs...what are you phoning for? To tell me off?"

"No, to let you know we've secured someone to do the drug drop."

"Who is it?"

"As it happens, it's Austin."

"I *beg* your pardon?"

"We'd asked him before this theft shitshow played out, so keep your wig on. As you engineered it so he'd nick your cash—fake notes, we know that, by the way—then as it isn't his fault because you put temptation in his way, knowing his situation, I'd like to use him regardless."

"But he *stole*," she said. "No matter that Satin encouraged him, he could have said no."

"But he was desperate."

"I know."

"And you took advantage of that. Look, he's a good bloke, just got himself into a bit of debt with Benny Bender, that's all."

Satin took a notepad out of her pocket and scribbled something down.

"Are you still there?" George asked.

"Yes, I was just thinking." India read the note: AGREE TO USE HIM. YOU CAN NAB HIM LATER ONCE HE'S BROUGHT THE DRUGS. She sighed at how beautifully Satin complemented her way of thinking. "Okay, you win. I'll play nicely now."

"Glad to hear it. As for Faith…"

"You want to deal with her, is that what you're implying? I rather thought your Cheshire would have stopped her from misbehaving, but it seems she didn't heed your warning. I'm really not happy about letting *both* of them go."

"But Satin told Austin to use Faith, so it's part of your silly game. If he hadn't approached her, she would never have done it. Don't you see how unfair that is? Listen, I get it, you need some fun in your life, but really?"

"We regularly put temptation in my employees' way to cut the wheat from the chaff. She's been working for me for *years*, and she stole what she thought was thousands of pounds. Call it a test of her loyalty, and she failed. I should be the one to deal with her. You can keep Austin, I don't care about him" —*liar*— "but don't expect me to give Faith up. I want you to pass it on to Austin that he must deliver her cut to her later when she's finished work."

"Let us deal with her."

"Come on now, you can't tell me you *want* the woman to enjoy life when she was so cruel to

Becky. She deserves to die for what she did, and I have a feeling you'd just kneecap her next instead of taking her out. I'm not afraid to do that."

"I see your point."

"Good, so she's mine, end of. So what time should I expect Austin with the cargo?"

"Ten o'clock."

"Wonderful. Goodbye!" She ended the call and placed her phone on the table. "He's going soft."

"Hmm. How will you explain why Austin's gone missing?"

"Easily. I'll say he gave me the drugs and left."

"George, especially, won't believe that, not when he knows you were after Austin in the first place. Would it be better for me to set someone else up instead so your mind's on that?"

India's heart sank. "That would be a shame. We've just had our celebratory waffles…"

Satin shrugged. "Fair enough. I'm with you whatever you decide to do."

"You're a good girl." India smiled.

"Promise me you'll get out," Errol said. "This life, it isn't for you. Your dad making sure you took the estate on when it was supposed to go to someone else…he was wrong. The other leaders were wrong for agreeing to it, too. I hate having my name associated with that place. You should have run it as your maiden name, Benson."

She'd thought of that but had dismissed it, too proud that she'd claimed his name when they'd married. A stupid move, now she came to think of it, as it had given her enemies a clue as to who she'd married, who to look for if they wanted to gun him down to hurt her. She hadn't kept him as safe as she'd thought.

She stared at him in his deathbed, hooked up to monitors, tubes coming out of his arms. He'd come home from hospital to die, wanting to go with familiar things around him. Tears pricked her eyes. He'd always said she didn't belong in the world of gangsters, that the real her was too kind and thoughtful to ever fit—but she'd only ever shown him *the real side of her, the only person she'd trusted to reveal it to. But she could flip a switch and become Mrs Whitehall, the woman who ran an estate with fists created from iron, only he never saw that.*

"It's what I've always done since the estate was passed to me. I can't do anything else."

"Think of all the money, what you could do with it. There are so many people you could help."

She could, and already did. She regularly donated to the Sickle Cell Society, and she funded a youth club for underprivileged minority kids, many of them black. Errol had run it for her until he'd become too poorly.

"You're going to turn towards hate when I'm gone," he whispered, struggling to get the words out, his breathing laboured.

"You know me well. And how can I not? You're my whole world. Without you, what have I got but anger? I hate that this disease is taking you away from me. It's unfair. You don't deserve to die."

"The Lord has chosen me. It's time for me to go home."

"But this is your home, not Heaven. For fuck's sake, Errol, you belong with me, not the fucking angels." She regretted her outburst immediately. This wasn't how she wanted things to go, an argument when he was so close to death. "I'm sorry, but I don't think you understand how much I love you."

"Then show me: do what I ask and get out. Let whoever's next take over the estate. Go off and do all *the things we thought we were going to do. Take me with you in your heart."*

She nodded. "I will." And she meant it in that moment. Letting go of her estate wouldn't be so bad, but grief would take her badly this time. It was all very well gadding about the world, visiting Jamaica and numerous other places on their list of destinations—if she wasn't filled with vitriol. But she knew all too well how she'd go when he left her because she'd dived into a pit of hate once her mother and father had passed. She'd railed against the world, killed people for minor misdemeanours.

She loved Errol more than she'd loved her parents, so there was no hope for her. She'd turn into the Devil himself and wreak as much havoc as possible behind the scenes. Not publicly, she couldn't afford for the other leaders to think she was unstable, them voting her out, taking her estate away. But perhaps a few games wouldn't hurt.

"I'll hand over the estate after the funeral," she lied.

Errol's smile, not quite resembling the one she'd fallen in love with because it was too sad, too lax, made a valiant attempt to light up his face.

"You deserve to be happy," he said, "not fucked up."

She didn't think so. The things she'd done, things he didn't know about, things she'd ordered. He had no idea who he'd married. She'd had to hide that side of her from him in order to keep him. Always a diamond on the outside, was Mrs Whitehall, but inside was another matter.

As if her vow to him had been all he'd hung on for, he closed his eyes and drifted away, his last exhale warming her chin as she kissed his forehead. Already the rage burned, and she held his hand until it lost its warmth, then got up to phone the palliative nurse who'd been visiting daily. In a daze, she went through the motions on autopilot, the two sides of her working simultaneously—one dealing with Errol's passing, the other plotting to bring a scrote in who'd been a pain in her neck for a few weeks now.

Yes, she'd enjoy killing him.

"Are you okay?" Satin asked.

India snapped out of the past. "Oh, yes, yes, I'm fine."

Her promise to Errol chewed on her conscience, but she brushed it off and stood.

"Go and see Bungle," she ordered. "Tell him what needs to be done. And I've changed my mind. I'll only take Austin to the abattoir. Tell Bungle he can do whatever he wants to Faith, I want nothing more to do with her."

See, Errol? I can be nice sometimes.

Chapter Sixteen

George drove towards the Goose and Gander, Greg in the passenger seat. The former Golden Eye Estate no longer had that ugly gold statue on the border, an eyesore that had blighted the view and blinded drivers if the sun was shining, reminding everyone that Goldie had been off his rocker by erecting a monument based on himself in the first place. Egotistical tosser.

Prince must have had it pulled down, which was only right, considering what a monstrosity it had been. How had the local council allowed it?

Goldie paid someone off, I bet.

George turned into the car park of the pub, drawing their BMW to a stop in front of the largest window. Diners and drinkers stared out, some of them realising who'd come to visit. Eyebrows up. Frowns down. The infamous car had announced their presence to Prince before they'd even got out of the car.

"Let's sit for a bit to let our arrival sink in," George said. "Get him wondering what the fuck we want."

"He'll be going through everything in his head to see if he's fucked up somewhere with us, and he'll be smirking while he does it an' all. Always was a smarmy fucker, so if he looks at me funny, I'm just warning you I might get arsey. I can't stand breathing the same air as him."

"Yeah, he's always a know-it-all at leader meetings, but you've got to hand it to him, he played his part well when we confronted Goldie at the warehouse."

"Only because he knew he'd be taking over his estate. He had a vested interest in doing what we suggested."

George couldn't argue with that. All of the leaders killing one of their own didn't happen often, only if the fallen leader had done something particularly shitty to another estate manager. Goldie had plotted to rob their casino, so he'd deserved to die via multiple bullets belonging to his peers. It got George thinking about Whitehall and whether they could trust her. She'd wanted Austin as her catch, to mete out her form of justice, but George had persuaded her to let him go. She'd given her word that she'd only nab Faith, so if she reneged on her promise regarding Austin, was that enough for all the leaders to haul her over the coals?

There were so many rules between leaders, and punishment was clear—fuck one of them over, and you paid the price. Did George want to fix Austin so much that he was prepared to dob a leader in because she'd taken his project away?

Probably. He was fickle like that.

Sad, this, as George had always thought Whitehall was a diamond, one of the best women he knew—apart from the games she played, but he'd put those down to grief. One mourner to another, he got it, understood. She'd been ace in the Goldie debacle. But she'd shown a different side to her earlier, one that hadn't painted her in a good light, and it had contaminated his view of her. Once the rot set in with someone, he found it hard to shift it.

"Come on."

They got out of the car. George hadn't phoned ahead to let Prince know they were coming—he wasn't fond of the prick, and annoying him by just turning up would tickle his pickle.

He led the way inside, mindful he had to show *some* respect by not broadening his shoulders and presenting as confrontational. If any leader did that when going into The Angel to find him and Greg, it'd get his back up and he'd want to shoot them in the nuts.

Prince sat with a couple of burly men in a raised booth so he could preside over the customers. He didn't own the pub but acted as if he did.

No different to how I am in The Angel.

At least George could see his own faults these days and accept them without getting sulky about it, but Prince wasn't one for admitting he'd done anything wrong, so George anticipated a prickly meeting.

Prince spotted them, and a quick frown gave away his true feelings. The smile that spread to replace it was supposed to get them thinking he was fine with them being there, but his emotions had already betrayed him. At least George knew where they stood.

And at least I have a poker face so he doesn't know where he stands. Yet.

He walked up to the dais casually, Greg right behind him.

"Is it okay to talk business?" George asked — being polite to this bloke churned his guts, but as in all businesses, there were some colleagues you just couldn't get along with yet you followed the rules.

"You didn't message to set up a meeting." Prince scowled and ran a hand through his hair. "It's only respectful to do that."

But you don't deserve respect. "We were out this way so thought we'd drop in on the off chance." George reckoned pacifying Prince with a lie would get them what they wanted, so he continued with, "Got to check if someone's lying to us or not, and you're the bloke to tell us."

Prince's demeanour changed, and he shooed his men away, a fat ruby ring glinting on his skinny finger. They slunk off to the bar, keeping an eye on the proceedings as if George ought to be afraid of them. He'd only have to say "Boo!" and they'd shit themselves. Still, if they wanted to maintain the illusion they were hard and of some use in the fist department, he wasn't going to deny them that pleasure.

He took the three steps up the dais and raised his eyebrows to ask if they could sit. Prince acted like royalty, and to park your arse without permission got on his nerves. Ruffian awoke inside George and prodded him to sit anyway, but he resisted.

Prince wafted a hand, and George sat opposite. Greg stood beside him.

"Are my seats not good enough for you, Greg?" Prince asked.

"No."

George held back a splutter of laughter, and Prince's scowl came back.

"Fucking rude of you," the leader said.

"I'm not here to ponce about," Greg replied. "We've got shit to do, so sitting here having a drink isn't on my agenda."

Prince studied him. "I didn't offer you a drink. It's not like you to be so abrasive. It's usually your brother. Maybe I don't want to talk to people if they've come here with a cunt-sized chip on their shoulder."

Oh, he didn't say that to my brother... George clenched his fists under the table. *He fucking did.*

"Then maybe you should keep yourself in check more," Greg threw back.

Prince narrowed his eyes. "What are you getting at?"

"We could have called for a leader meeting over this." Greg let that hang in the air. "But we're giving you the courtesy of sorting it out on the quiet."

"Sorting what out?"

Greg planted his hands on the table and leaned forward. "Letting someone from your estate fuck about with someone on ours."

"Letting?" Prince's eyebrows hiked up. "I doubt that very much."

"Benny Bender."

Prince smiled. "Ah, Mr Hunt went running to you two, did he? All Benny was doing ensuring the man paid up on time. He gets so many people who promise to stick to the agreement then let him down. He's just protecting his investment."

Greg's jaw twitched. "You didn't do your due diligence and tell Benny not to go round Austin's gaff. He sent heavies at first, then turned up himself. Austin's agreed to pay back what Benny wants, but he asked for more. He came to see you about it."

"Who did?"

"Don't play dumb, I'm not in the mood. Austin told you what Benny was doing, and you said the lender was legit so it wasn't your problem." Greg moved his head closer. "But it *is* your problem when he's been on our estate, playing the hardman."

Prince nodded. "I suppose I'd be naffed off it the tables were turned. I'll tell Benny to back off."

Greg cocked his head. "No need. We're here to warn you that he'll be taken care of. You know how it goes. He broke the rules on our estate, so he's ours to punish."

George thought about Mrs Whitehall again— she had a point about Austin and Faith being hers, yet here they were, acting out double standards. They hadn't allowed Mrs Whitehall that privilege where Austin was concerned.

We're hypocrites.

George shrugged that off—something to ponder another day. "My brother's right. Benny's ours."

Prince nodded again. "He was getting on my tits anyway. Poncing around threatening *my* people, too. I just hadn't got around to pulling him up on it, so do what you will." A glimmer of malice flitted over his rat-like face. "I'll take over his business. Do me a favour and get him to tell you who all his clients are if he hasn't got them written down, will you?"

Greg pushed off the table and straightened. "You want *us* to do your dirty work? Like we're your skivvies?"

"It would be kind of you to do so." Prince smiled.

"Fucking lazy bastard." Greg stalked out.

George stood. "He's got a wasp up his arse for some reason. Sorry about that." He wasn't sorry, he found it fucking funny, but it didn't hurt to feign being polite, did it.

Prince smiled. "You're doing me a favour now I come to think of it, so I'll let Greg's behaviour slide. As in, *I* won't call for a leader meeting to discuss his attitude, giving *you* the courtesy of sorting it out on the quiet."

Nicely played, but you don't have the right air of menace about you, sunshine, so your threat fell flat.

"Cheers." George took ten grand out of his inner suit pocket and slapped the envelope on the table. "This is more than what Austin owes Benny—if you're taking over the business, the cash belongs to you. Austin will be paying *us* back now. This ends here. He's left alone."

Prince took the envelope. "I don't want to see him on my estate again, asking for loans, understand? This little debacle may have dropped a lucrative business in my lap, but I really don't like the hassle it's caused. I prefer peace. Harmony."

George held in a snort—*who's he trying to kid?*—and strutted out, Ruffian asking if he could slit Prince's throat while he slept in his big house on top of a hill. A castle of sorts, four chimneys as turrets. George was surprised the prick didn't have a moat.

Would the other leaders care if Prince happened to pass away?

He doubted it. Not many liked him, he was tolerated. He didn't run his estate very well, and it seemed since he'd taken over Golden Eye, he'd bitten off more than he could chew with the extra work. All that peace and harmony bollocks translated to Prince being lazy.

Outside, George headed for the BMW and got in. Buckled up. "What the fuck was that all about?"

"I did warn you." Greg propped his elbow on the door and rested his cheek in his hand. "He got on my nips, sitting there like a king. I've never liked him."

"Ruffian wants him sorted."

Greg shifted his eyes George's way. "Does Ruffian want me to go with him?"

George shook his head. "I don't want you involved if I decide to go ahead. Killing a leader just because he gets on our wick... Ramifications. One of us needs to be on hand to run Cardigan if I get caught, so I'd rather be the one taking the risk."

"You can't coddle me forever, bruv."

George started the engine. "I think you'll find I can. I'll *always* keep you out of harm's way if possible. Besides, he implied you're a cunt. He needs to pay for that."

"I bloody love you, cockwomble."

"Love you, too. Now stop being an emotional fanny. We've got work to do. Fuck going to The Naked Fountain, we'll go to Benny's now. I've got excess energy to burn."

Chapter Seventeen

*L*ife after rape was harder than Faith had imagined. Every morning, she woke with a sense of dread that she had to face another day wading through the quagmire, and every night, she waited for some man to break in and come into her room. Wreck her all over again. Put her through hell all over again.

Two years had passed. Since fourteen, she'd been blighted by her ordeal, her mind twisted even further *than it'd been before by images of what Tim had done. Not only did she carry her father's spite in her bones, the fires of which she stoked regularly, but she hefted Tim's perversion around with her, deep in the marrow, so deep she'd never be able to get it out. Mum said she was ruined now, spoiled like bad milk, that no one would want her, and if she thought she could dupe someone into thinking she was a virgin, she'd better think again. Men knew, she'd said, men were aware when a woman tried to trick them.*

It seemed women were less aware when it came to men tricking them, *though. Or Mum was anyway. Faith saw it all clear as day, how Mum had been taken in by that bastard. Tim violating her had opened Faith's mind up, sharpened her vision, and she viewed things so differently now. She hoped she'd never change in that regard, never allow a man to cloud her thoughts. The idea of that horrified her. She'd always be in control—always. Falling in love wasn't for her, especially if it turned her into someone like Mum who couldn't see the wood for the trees no matter how close the trunks were in front of her.*

Faith didn't want a relationship, to have sex ever again. That one time was enough. Just the thought of it had her breaking out in hives. They cropped up on her arms now, and she scratched the hot red pimples until they bled.

"You're doing that for attention," Mum said and slammed Faith's dinner down on the table. A few peas jumped off the plate and fell on the floor. "Why can't you just get on and pretend it never happened? I mean, not only did you make sure my boyfriend got taken away by the police when you went and told on him, you're still going on about it now, drawing it out, wanting the limelight. Get a grip and behave like a normal teenager, for God's sake!"

Funny how Mum had changed so much. How, when Dad had been alive, infesting Faith's mind with his racist rants, Mum had told him how wrong he was, yet with Tim, she couldn't see how wrong he'd been. She didn't want to. Didn't want to believe he'd touched Faith. She'd implied the sperm left inside her belonged to someone else, a lad she'd had sex with on the quiet, and so she didn't get into trouble, Faith had blamed Tim, an 'easy target'. Tim had admitted it, he'd been put away for a few years, yet Mum still went around blinkered, refusing to accept it. And also, why was it okay for Mum to tell the police about Dad but not for Faith to reveal all about Tim?

Hypocrite.

"I won't ever forget it," Faith said. "It'll always be there."

"Then that's your lookout." Mum attacked her mash. "Just don't bring the subject up with me or within my earshot. You've embarrassed me enough as it is."

What had happened to Mum saying she wanted to be a decent role model to Faith? How had one man turned her into someone unrecognisable?

It had been in the papers, Tim's name mentioned and everything, and Mum had found it necessary to move out of their safe haven and go to the other side of the East End where she didn't know anyone. Faith had changed schools and been given the explicit instruction not to mention what had happened, it had to be a secret they'd never share.

Faith didn't want to share it, not yet, but maybe one day she would if she felt comfortable with someone. The shame was enough to cripple her as it was, let alone bringing more pressure down on her shoulders in the form of people either giving her pitying glances or staring at her like she'd asked for it. Why didn't anyone understand? Why was it the woman's fault, not the man's? The majority of the police she'd spoken to didn't see it that way. But one man had, Detective Stoddard, all narrowed eyes, suspicion lacing them.

He'd stared at her as though she were shit on his shoe. He'd suggested she'd slept in the nude, had tried to get her to say that, too, explaining it would be hard for any man to resist, her body basically on a platter. She'd told him about her nightie, how Tim must have lifted it while she'd slept.

"Then you should have worn knickers and a bra," he'd said. "All these girls out in short skirts and tops that show off their chests. Is it any wonder men are tempted? It's like putting a bowl of Pedigree Chum down for a dog and expecting him not to eat it."

He'd said this while they'd been alone, and she'd told the nice policewoman about it, PC Jones, but nothing had been done, even though Jones had reported him. A sexist force, it seemed, something Faith had had no knowledge of until then.

"Some men feel a woman gets what she deserves if they're flaunting it," Jones had said. "What I think is that it's the men's responsibility to keep their penises to themselves — and you should think the same. Don't ever let anyone tell you this was your fault. You're a minor, and that man should never have gone into your bedroom. He had no right — and it wouldn't be right even if you weren't underage."

It was one thing to think that but another to truly believe it. Faith struggled, asking herself if she'd touched Tim in a way that had given him the wrong idea—brushing past him on the way to the toilet or something. Or had she said something he'd taken as flirting? There was nothing. She'd kept out of his way for the most part because of how he'd looked at her since she'd turned thirteen and her breasts had appeared. He'd stared at them, and she'd vowed to keep herself skinny forever so they'd never get bigger.

"I suspect he chose her mother because she had a daughter," PC Jones had mused with another copper after the initial interview, not seeming worried Faith could hear her—or perhaps she thought she couldn't. "Men like him, they prey on women with children. She said she was young when he came on the scene—he has all the trademarks of a pervert wanting to groom."

Groom? What did that mean?

Later, Jones had asked Faith, "Now then, how do you feel about counselling?"

Mum had vetoed it. Said Faith didn't need to spill her guts to some stranger. Faith had wanted to go, she'd been desperate to understand how this had happened, how she felt afterwards, and how she should feel going forward. Instead of the help she so needed, she'd muddled along alone, only bringing it up occasionally with Mum, and now she'd put a stop to that with what she'd just said.

172

"Wipe the slate clean and start again," Mum went on. "Oh, and I must get down to M and S and pick up some trousers for Tim. I'll take them in when I next visit him. Shall I send him your regards?"

"No, he can fuck off to Hell," Faith said and stabbed one of her sausages, wishing it was his dick.

"Language!" Mum admonished.

Faith couldn't believe this. How was Mum so...so into Tim after what he'd done?

"You're thick as shit," Faith raged. "He admitted it in court, and there's you, gadding about like he didn't do anything. What's wrong with you?"

Mum got up and came closer so her nose almost touched Faith's. She braced her hands on the table. "I've had enough heartache in my life with your father, thank you very much, and I deserve happiness with Tim. I had it until you lured him into your room."

"I didn't lure him in. And you want happiness with a rapist?"

"It was a mistake, one he regrets. You have to forgive if you're going to get any peace."

"I'll never forgive him. He's an animal."

"Then you're going to end up a very bitter and twisted woman."

"Rather that than a deluded one."

Faith walked out and upstairs to the bedroom that still seemed as though it wasn't hers. This house didn't feel like home and maybe never would.

She couldn't wait for the day she could leave forever.

At eighteen, Faith found a factory job and moved into a bedsit in a shared house. The freedom was unlike anything she'd imagined—she came and went as she pleased, no Mum loitering, ready to ask questions or berate her for still 'moping around' about the rape. Faith hadn't been to see her for three months and didn't want to. Life was so much easier without the angst that came with her mother.

She sat in the living room with two of the other residents, an old man called Bailey (could be his surname, she'd never asked), and Mina who'd run away from an abusive home. Both of them had helped Faith heal a little—she'd shared her secret in a moment of drunken weakness, fuck what Mum had said about keeping it to herself.

"Bloody weather's on the turn," Bailey grumbled and eyed the rain droplets on the window. "Winter's going to be a bad one, you see if I'm not right." His

wife had chucked him out because of his drinking, and he lived in the attic space that had been done out as a flat. "I hope that landlord of ours gets the heating fixed soon. Fucking freezing in here last year, it was."

"I only have one blanket," Faith said, worry cresting inside her. She didn't earn that much, and forking out for more bedding would leave her short.

"I've got a spare quilt you can have," Mina said.

"Thank you."

If Mum had been a nicer person, she'd have given Faith more than one blanket to take to her new digs. Parents had a lot to answer for, she'd learned that, because Mina's had treated her like shit, and she had a serious fear of wasps because her dad used to put them in jam jars by her bed, holes in the lid to keep them alive, because he knew the buzzing scared her.

The three of them had demons, ones they discussed so it didn't send them mad, and for the first time in her life, Faith felt properly accepted. That was a lie, she'd been accepted at Sally and Clinton's, but she couldn't bring herself to acknowledge that.

"Are you racist?" she blurted. Her cheeks heated. Why the hell had she said that? To see if they were, too, so she'd be accepted even more? "I mean, my dad brought me up to hate blacks and all that, and I wondered—"

"They don't belong here," Bailey said. "I bloody hate the sight of them."

"Hmm." Mina twirled a hank of her blonde hair around a finger. "They ought to just fuck off, back to where they came from."

Faith thought about Clinton and what he'd told her. That he'd been born here, so where else was he supposed to go? Once again, confusion swirled inside her. Here she was, with people who thought the same as Dad, and yet…

"Bastards," she said to solidify Dad's teachings in her mind.

"There's one moved in down the road." Bailey sucked in his bottom lip. "There's been a right uproar about it. Since he came, people have been getting their stuff nicked. It doesn't take much to work it out, does it."

Faith hadn't seen the man in question. She got up early for the factory and did overtime so arrived home late. "My dad couldn't stand them, said they were thieves and liars."

"They are," Bailey confirmed. "Take him along the street for example. A whole load of neighbours confronted him about the shit going missing, and he denied it. Yeah, he's a liar all right. We should beat the fucker up when he leaves his house, drive him out."

"I'll organise it if you like," Mina said. "I've got nothing on this weekend. We could do it Saturday."

The light of malice lit Bailey's eyes, and he grinned, showing his tobacco-stained teeth. "He goes down the Flag of a Saturday, chatting up all our women. A load of us could go down there and wait for him at kicking-out time. Give him a different kind of kicking."

Faith imagined it, all those people against one man. She should feel bad, considering Dad had killed someone the same way, but she wanted to feel what he had, to experience the rage, then the relief at doing something about those kinds of people. She wanted to be just like him. Maybe then it would bring his memory closer.

She was starting to forget his face, his smile, his voice, and it frightened her.

Outside the Flag, Faith huddled with twenty-three neighbours in an alley beside the pub. Her breath gusted out in clouds, and she rubbed her gloved hands together to get warmth from the friction. Mina had had organised everything, her dander up, adrenaline high. Most here had a score to settle with Tarone

Campbell—they'd all had things stolen, they all wanted justice.

Several customers had already left, some going past the alley, like Tarone would, the others walking across the street and disappearing into the darkness. Faith's nerves couldn't take this—a part of her knew this was wrong, Mum's voice bleating on that Tarone was a man like any other and didn't deserve to be called a thief when he wasn't. Dad's voice, on the other hand, matched Bailey's and urged her to see this through until the end.

The creak of the pub door opening screeched through the night, and everyone held their breath. A man in a trilby walked by, head bent, hands in his jeans pockets, a short sheepskin coat keeping him warm.

"That's my fucking coat!" Ollie said. "I wondered where that had gone, thought I'd left it down the pub. It's even got a slit in the sleeve like mine. You can't tell me he didn't nick it. That's it, I'm going for him."

The plan had been to wait until Tarone got to the park entrance down the way a bit, so deviating could fuck it all up—if Ollie blasted down the street after him now, they risked residents seeing them beating the shit out of him.

"Wait," Bailey said. "We follow in one minute. Stick to what we said."

Ollie huffed. "I'm that angry…"

"What if Tarone didn't nick the coat? What if someone else did and he bought if off them?" *Mum's voice again.*

"It was him." *Dad.* "Too much of a coincidence."

Faith kept her thoughts to herself. She'd found a family in Bailey and Mina and didn't want to ruin it. Here was her chance to be someone, to be a part of something important, making a stand.

"Right, let's go," Bailey said. "Remember, walk quietly. We don't want him to know we're behind him."

Faith waited for everyone else to file out then tagged onto the end of the incensed crowd. She thought of Dad killing himself because he couldn't face up to murdering Arvinda; would she feel the same with Tarone? She could back out now, this was the ideal chance to walk away, but her new friends would notice she'd gone and might give her the cold shoulder in future. No, she had to see this through. She hadn't been given a specific job to do tonight, she didn't have to kick him like everyone else, she could just stand and watch, but she had to be there if she wanted to remain pally with this lot.

The park entrance loomed, and Bailey raised a hand, the signal for them to leave stealth mode and run hell for leather at Tarone, sod any noise they made now they'd gone past the houses. Everyone sped up, and Faith moved to the side of the pavement to see better. Tarone glanced over his shoulder, spotted the mob, and legged it.

"Get the bastard!" Bailey ordered.

Tarone had gone past the park.

Someone sprinted faster than everyone else and tackled Tarone to the ground, dragging him back to the entrance, the darkness swallowing them up. Faith hurried with the others, through the gateway and onto the path that led to the swings. She couldn't see a thing until someone switched a torch on and aimed the spotlight at the grass ahead. Tarone, thrown to the ground, curled up into a ball and covered his head. He'd anticipated what was about to happen—had he experienced this sort of thing before?

The neighbours created a circle around him, and Faith squeezed in beside Mina and Ollie. One by one, each person stepped into the ring and kicked Tarone, laughter and rumbles of encouragement rising into the night. Faith flinched with every attack, seeing him as a person being beaten, nothing else. A well of mixed-up feelings swirled inside her, and she dithered, dreading her turn one minute, relishing it the next.

Mina elbowed her in the side. "Your go."

Faith stepped into the ring and approached a crying Tarone who swore blind he hadn't stolen anything in his life and there'd been a mistake.

"Where did you get my fucking coat from, then?" Ollie seethed.

Tarone, still shielding his head, said, "Off that man who goes down the market."

"A likely story," Ollie muttered.

Faith swallowed and went closer. Was this what Dad had felt like as he'd gone up to Arvinda, this…this heady rush of euphoria twinned with anger surging through him? Buoyed up by the jeering, she drew her leg back then let her foot fly forward. She kicked Tarone in the side of the head, the force of the impact jarring up her shin. The toe of her stiletto split the skin, and someone laughed so hard it only encouraged her to do it again. She aimed, struck the same place, and blood flowed.

"That's it, Faith girl," Bailey said, "make the fucker bleed."

Faith reversed. Mina moved to stand by their victim.

Blood pumping, disgust for Tarone heating her body, Faith watched in fascination. Mina, in her heavy bovver boots, let rip, Tarone crying out, his voice hoarse.

Faith should look away. She should be ashamed.

But as she'd known would be the case, she wasn't.

Instead, she smiled.

Chapter Eighteen

Benny Bender sat behind his desk in his Portakabin and reclined, hands linked over his midriff. He'd just eaten a large meal from the chippy, the three Pukka pies sitting heavy in his hard, distended gut. Must be the gluten. He wasn't meant to eat that. Two of his men, Roger and Jerry, poured brandies from the crystal carafe then came to sit opposite.

Roger pushed Benny's glass over. "I'm fucking knackered."

Benny smiled. "Takes it out of you, beating the shit out of someone."

A woman hadn't followed the rules, her payment a couple of hours late, and Benny had given the order to teach her a little lesson. He didn't give a fuck *what* gender people were, if they broke the agreement, they suffered the consequences. She currently resided in the hospital, an ambulance arriving to collect her after a good Samaritan had swooped in and saved the day. Roger and Jerry had attacked her in the street, blending into a shadowed alley afterwards to watch the proceedings. The woman, Tarty Tanya, an aging slag of the highest order, hooked on heroin, had promised not to grass them up, but Benny was on alert anyway. The pigs could catch her at a weak moment, then come storming round here to arrest them.

"You're better off keeping a low profile for a bit in her area," Benny said. "I take it you had balaclavas on."

"Yeah." Roger picked fish out of his teeth. "We parked the car streets away, fake plates an' all that, then ditched it in a field. Set the fucker on fire."

Benny, satisfied they had their arses covered, sat upright to sip some celebratory brandy. The burn went all the way down to meet the pies. "How long did you give her to catch up on the payments?"

"Seeing as we fucked her over good and proper—she'll be sucking soup out of a straw for a while—I gave her another month with three grand interest on top," Jerry said. "Maybe one of her richer clients will stump up the cash for her before then. That MP shags her on the regular. What's he called? William Barnaby, that's it."

"Maybe he needs to know we have pictures of him with her. The *Daily Mail* would be our best bet. Then I'll send a letter to his constituency office and demand the cash, letting him know we have more damaging pictures we can share with the world."

A knock at the door had Roger and Jerry jumping up and going to the blind-covered windows. They parted the wooden slats, peering out.

"Fuck," Roger muttered.

"Boys in blue?" Benny asked, a frisson of worry going through him.

"No, The Brothers."

Fuck indeed. What did *they* want?

"Let them in." Benny stood, gathering his mettle. He was a mean bastard, but those two had the ability to crush him before he could blink. His heart pulsed painfully—fear or indigestion? He'd blame it on indigestion. No way was he scared of those two.

Liar.

Roger opened the door and puffed himself up. The wrong move—the twins wouldn't appreciate it, but Benny hadn't had time to give them a warning on how to behave with that pair of nutters.

"You don't have an appointment," Roger stated.

Bloody hell, shut up before they clout you...

"Come in," Benny called then pasted on a smile.

Roger stepped back, and fucking hell, the twins came in, larger than Benny had realised. He'd seen them from a distance, but up close like this... They ate more than Weetabix for breakfast and clearly consumed a lot of spinach, going by their biceps. He chuckled at his joke then checked himself in case they took umbrage.

"What's so fucking funny?" one of them said.

Which was which? They appeared identical, right down to the clothes and the blue rubber gloves, although one had black shoes, the other brown. The brown didn't go well with the grey suit, but he'd keep that to himself.

The gloves gave him pause now he'd registered them properly. This wasn't a friendly visit.

"Funny?" Benny said. "I wasn't aware anyone laughed."

"You did," Black Shoes said. "Don't treat me like I'm stupid, sunshine."

"I apologise." Benny didn't like having to do that. He had quite the racket going on here, a king in his own little world, Prince backing him, so to be reminded that he was a minnow in a sea of piranhas didn't sit well.

"So you should." Black Shoes stared at Roger then Jerry. "Fuck off out of it."

Roger bristled and clenched his fists.

"I wouldn't bother." Brown Shoes squared up to him, a foot taller and wider than the man he glared at. "Prince knows we're here, and you'd be better off going to see him at the Goose and letting him know you need a new employer."

Benny barked out a nervous laugh, the implied message hitting him hard. If Roger and Jerry needed to go and see Prince…

Has he taken his protection away?

His arsehole spasmed, and he had to fight not to sit, his knees going weak. "What's going on?"

The twins ignored him, still in a staring standoff with Roger and Jerry.

Black Shoes took a gun out of his holster and planted the end on Jerry's forehead. "I've got no qualms about pulling this trigger, my old son, so if you want to push me, be my guest. My advice would be to do as you're told, be a good little boy and pay your leader a visit, because Benny here won't have a job for you anymore, but Prince will. Do you get what I'm saying?"

Jerry nodded and swivelled his eyes to Benny. "Sorry, boss…"

While Benny understood being on the business end of a gun was frightening, it bugged the shit out of him that Jerry saying sorry meant his loyalty only went so far. He'd have sworn the bloke would have fought for him, stood by him until the last knockings, but the bastard walked out.

Black Shoes raised his eyebrows at Roger. "What the fuck are *you* still doing here? Go on, sod off."

Roger glanced at Benny and fled, the door slamming behind him then bouncing back open. Brown Shoes closed it and slid the lock in place.

Black Shoes smiled. "I'm George Wilkes, just in case you were wondering. Now then, we've got a bone to pick with you."

Benny had an idea what that was, but he wasn't going to verbally fill in the blanks. Best to play dumb for now. "What's that then?"

"Like you don't know." Greg walked closer. "You've been a naughty boy."

George joined him, and faced with two brick shithouses in front of him, Benny didn't feel too well.

"Whatever I do has Prince's blessing," he said.

"Not anymore." George held his gun up. "Not now he knows you've been on our estate, paying Austin Hunt a visit. You know, we should really have shot those two pricks of yours in the knees, seeing as they were likely the ones to go and put the shits up Austin, but I suspect Prince wants to use them when he takes over your business."

"W-what?" Benny's façade threatened to crumble and show him up for the scared wanker he was. They were serious. Prince was going to hijack his world.

"You heard. Where's your client list?" George jerked the gun in the air. "And I'm not fucking about here. If you don't give it to me, I've got no problem with shooting you in the toe, then then shin, then the thigh...you get the gist. The last bullet will be in your head."

Benny glanced at his desk drawer. "In there."

"Get it out and hand it to my brother."

Hands shaking, Benny withdrew the ledger with one hand and grabbed his gun from beside it with the other. Dropping the ledger on the desk to distract them, he whipped the gun up and fired.

A second gunshot ricocheted around the cabin straight after his, and a spear of pain erupted in Benny's stomach. A bullet or the pies giving him gyp? He dropped his gun, stared down at his belly. A red stain spread on his white shirt, and fiery heat seeped across his skin.

"What a knob," Greg said. "You shot *between* us, you dickhead."

George came round the desk and gripped the back of Benny's suit jacket, dragging him round to the other side. "I can't work out which one of us you were stupid enough to try and shoot, but I'll take it that you meant to hurt my brother. *No one* hurts him, and because you had a good go, I'm even more angry than I was before." He shoved Benny against one of the windows, the Venetian blind clattering. "I had planned to just beat you up, give you a Cheshire as a warning not to come to our estate and play the big man, but I've changed my mind."

Benny stared at the hole in the end of the gun, raised so it aimed between his eyes. "Please, I won't go there again. Fuck, my guts are killing me."

"No, *I'm* killing you." George's smile turned maniacal.

Benny closed his eyes and waited.

Chapter Nineteen

George listened to the final echo of the gunshot and let Benny slump to the floor. He snatched a bunch of keys out of the wally's pocket and nodded to Greg. They left, George dropping the keys under the cabin so Prince could get in, although anyone who wanted entry would have no trouble now the bullet had gone through Benny's head and splintered the window.

In the car, he put the gun in the glove box and stripped off his gloves, leaving them inside out. Greg would burn them at home later.

George smiled at his brother getting into the passenger seat. "Thought we'd leave him as a present for Prince instead of carting him back to the warehouse for chopping."

Greg nodded. "We'll ditch the guns to be on the safe side—bullets and casings have been left behind."

"Yep." George took his leader burner out and messaged Prince.

GG: Benny's no longer a problem to us, but you need to dispose of him. Client ledger on his desk at his cabin. You're welcome.

Prince: I wasn't aware you were killing him! I thought you'd just rough him up. I had no clue I had to get rid of him.

GG: I just told you, so now you *are* aware.

Prince: Thanks for nothing.

GG: We just handed a business to you on a plate. Be grateful.

Prince: [middle finger emoji]

George showed Greg the screen. "D'you know, he's boiling my fucking piss."

"You're definitely going to end him now, aren't you?"

George smiled and put the phone in the cupholder. "Yep. He's disrespectful."

Greg closed his eyes. "Just be careful, all right?"

Nodding, George drove away, allowing Ruffian to offer other suggestions on how to kill Prince. The slitting of his throat was still the most appealing, so he'd go with that. Moon was in line to take over Prince's estate, so their good friend would be grumpy. He was getting on in years and likely wouldn't want the equivalent of two extra estates, Judas and Golden Eye.

"Text Moon and forewarn him he's got a manor coming his way at some point so he's got time to mull over whether he accepts it or not. Tell him to keep it under his hat and we'll explain later."

Greg picked up the phone.

"Oh, and message Prince and let him know that money I spotted in the bin by the desk is fake."

"Nah, let him find out for himself."

George laughed but quickly sobered. With Benny out of the way, Austin was safe, but there was still the dilemma of what to do with him in the long run. His story had sounded genuine enough, but George no longer trusted his gut instinct when it came to tales that could be taller than the Shard.

"Do you think Austin's really on the level?" he asked. "*Did* he only do what Satin wanted because he was desperate, or was he being greedy?"

Greg finished texting Moon and sighed. "I believed him."

"Glad you said that, because I do, too, but I was worried I was going soft again."

"He's got himself in a mess, that's all. We'll keep tabs on him for a while, make sure he's kosher. If he isn't… Well, you know what to do — despite him being your project. You can't fix everyone."

"We all make mistakes, and he didn't do anything to us, so…"

"He wronged Mrs Whitehall, though, and he coerced Faith into stealing for him, so technically, he *did* do something to us by approaching one of our residents. Albeit a bitch we hate, but still…"

"But only because he was out of his mind with worry." George had a sudden bad feeling; it swamped him so much he couldn't ignore it. "What if Whitehall goes against what we agreed and does something to him tonight when he drops the package off?"

"She wouldn't dare."

"Wouldn't she? Those sick games she brags about—she's not right in the head."

"Who is? Ruffian plays sick games. So does Mad."

"Fair enough."

Lately, George had got used to having a mirror held up in front of him. Vic had taught him not to get defensive about it, to study his reflection to see if he could be a better person instead of going with his knee-jerk reactions. It helped him maintain a handle on Mad and Ruffian, which was something he'd never wanted because he'd hadn't thought he was good enough as Just George—and he'd felt like something was missing when he'd tried to keep Mad locked up that time. The therapist had shown him different, and to George's surprise, he didn't mind the bloke he was inside, the caring part of him who didn't have to resort to violence. The man he might have become had they not been brought up with Richard and Ron Cardigan in their lives.

Would he fully be Just George when they retired? Could he let the other sides of himself go?

The question is, will they let me *go?*

What an uncomfortable thought, that he had no control of his personas, that they'd lived inside him for so long that they might not take kindly to being evicted. He reckoned they'd dig their heels in, maintain squatters' rights, and there wasn't a damn thing he could do about it.

They'd be with him until his dying day.

Chapter Twenty

Faith had spent hours at work in a state of apprehension, shitting herself every time someone knocked on her door, relieved when it was only Petra asking if she needed a drink or something to eat. Faith had twenty minutes to kill, her final punter not due yet, so she went to the staffroom. Shitty sat at the table having a cuppa, her usual habit prior to going home; she had to catch the Tube and reckoned she needed to wind down before she joined the crush in one of the carriages.

Faith made an English Breakfast tea, unable to stand any more coffee; the caffeine hit would add to her anxiety. Shitty launched into a diatribe about a woman who'd come into the shop, red-faced and embarrassed, asking for help with some bedroom toys.

"I mean, if you're in a sex shop, it's obvious what you're there to buy, isn't it, and we all know what she's going to do with the stuff she bought, so why get all silly about it?"

"Not everyone's comfortable letting people know what they want to get up to." Faith squeezed the teabag against the side of the cup, thinking back to Tim and what he'd done to her, how he'd ensured she was afraid to explore her sexuality because to her, sex had equalled rape, had equalled disgusting. Even with Reggie it hadn't been all hearts and flowers like some women said it was. He'd forced her to do things she didn't want to, dressing her up like a prostitute and getting her to behave like one. She hadn't known why at the time, but Jesus had she found out—he'd been getting her ready to send her out onto the streets.

She pushed the memories away. The past was such a bastard, keep barging into her head like this without her calling on it. Lemon's death had unlocked the box she'd hidden everything in. Was that what being left on your own did? Opened the floodgates? Forced you to face who you'd been, who you were, and who you could be? She'd wanted to do that, but these unbidden flashbacks weren't on.

Faith sighed. "The poor cow probably felt ashamed."

"I suppose we're so used to all things sex that we don't stop to think how others feel."

"*You* clearly didn't," Faith snapped. She turned to Shitty, shirking off her old self and climbing into the person she wished she was, who she wanted to be. "Sorry, it's been a tough time. I didn't mean to bark at you."

"Yeah, must have been tough losing Lemon, not to mention all that stuff about him in the paper. Running round with the Sparrow Lot and everything."

No need to rub it in. Faith successfully kept that to herself, although the words, heavy on her tongue, begged to come out. Her go-to had been lashing out for so long that it was second nature, and keeping it reined in was harder than she'd thought it would be. "What he did was on him. I won't take the blame for his actions."

Although she should. She'd brought him up wrong. With no proper influence to steady her ship, she'd turned into a nasty person and, in turn, had manipulated Lemon the same way as her father had done with her. They said the cycle of abuse continued into the next generation if you didn't stamp it out quick enough. She *should* have stopped it, but her hatred had been so deep that she'd let it ruin her son. She'd wanted him to love her, to come to her for advice, to be his all, to have someone who loved her unconditionally, and by doing that, she'd actually pushed him farther away.

"Actually, scrub that," she said. "While I didn't tell him to go round with the Sparrows, I did tell him he could do whatever he wanted, when he wanted, so it *is* my fault." It hadn't been so difficult to admit that out loud after all, but it still burned.

"How have you been, though? I mean, losing your kid…"

"It was awful, but I'll get through it."

Shitty stood and put her empty cup in the sink. "Suppose I'd better battle the masses. It's my day off tomorrow, thank God, so I'll get a lie-in." She picked her bags up off the table and walked to the door. "I bought both of those sets of lingerie. My boyfriend's going to wet himself. Tarra."

Faith waved absently, wishing she was Shitty, living a simple life. Her mind turned to the money and what she'd done to get it. She hadn't dared go out to the bin and see if Austin had collected the cash, but she'd wanted to. He hadn't replied to her message either, which was worrying. What if he'd fucked off with her cut? She'd be stuck working here to earn enough to make her escape, fretting every second that Mrs Whitehall knew about it but was biding her time before dishing out a punishment. How come the alarm hadn't been raised? Why hadn't Vanda or Mrs Whitehall spotted the cash missing from the safe?

She remembered she still had the last two clients' payments to put in there; she'd been too antsy to return to Len's office in case she walked in on someone just as they discovered the empty safe. Her acting skills might have let her down.

She'd have to go and do it now, though; Vanda had gone home, so passing it to her wasn't an option.

She quickly drank her tea then swilled the cup out in the sink. In the corridor, she took the money from her bra and walked to Len's office. Inside, she added the client information to the spreadsheet and opened the safe.

Money filled both shelves.

She stared for a moment, shocked to see it, puzzled as to why the stacks were identical to the ones she'd nicked—they were in the same place as the last lot, right down to the pile without the elastic band. She placed the punters' cash on top of it, thinking she'd gone mad, that she hadn't stolen the money, had only dreamt it, because how the hell could it still *be* there?

Scared she'd lost her marbles, she locked the safe and left the room. In hers, she paced, recalling exactly what she'd done when she'd committed the robbery. Yes, she'd definitely done it, so was someone playing games? There was no way the shop had sold enough items for the stacks to be replaced so fast, and the amount of men visiting the brothel hadn't been the usual.

The buzzer sounded, giving Faith a jolt, and she went to the door to greet her client. An older black man stood there, his hair white at the temples, and it took her off guard for a second or two. Revulsion reared its ugly head inside her before she could stop it, and she battled to maintain her composure. Her preference form stated whites only, and it had never been a problem before, so why was someone like him standing there now? Petra knew damn well not ignore what was on the form.

Stop it. He's just a man.

"Oh, um, come in." She stepped back to allow him entry then stuck her head out into the corridor.

She stared down it to Petra's desk in reception, hoping the woman turned her way so she could mouth to her "What the fuck?", but Petra's head remained bowed.

Faith faced the man. "I won't be a second. Make yourself comfortable."

She marched down the corridor, hating having to cause a scene, but she wasn't far enough along on her journey to accept the man as a client. Then she thought of the robbery, how she'd draw attention to herself if she kicked up a fuss, and

Mrs Whitehall's words came back to remind her that she ought to just get on with it.

"...if I ever hear of you being racist again, I'll kill you."

Faith turned back around and entered her room.

"Nice to see you," he said, holding a hand out.

She shook it, and a shudder went through her. Thoughts of Dad filled her head, his cruel words circling, and she slapped on a smile to hide her emotions. She could do this, couldn't she? Prove that what he'd said was wrong and Mum had been right—this man *was* like any other, he just happened to have dark skin.

She let his hand go and closed the door. "I'm Faith. What would you like today?"

"Just to talk." He sat on the bed and smiled. "Maybe about St Thomas and the Jumbees if you have a mind. It's been a long time. Mrs Whitehall's men found me this afternoon, asked me to come."

She sagged against the door. "Clinton?"

Whitehall had poked into her past? Sent her blokes out to go nosing? And so quickly, too. Who had they spoken to? Who'd opened their mouths for a few quid in order for them to know about Clinton? Shit, that woman was cleverer than Faith had given her credit for. Why had she found him? Why had she sent him to Faith? To force her to be nice to him? To prove a point?

"I went there," he said. "Me and Sally, our boy, his wife, and our granddaughter, we went to St Thomas. A few months ago, it was."

She recalled his stories. Nostalgia wrapped itself around her. Mum and Dad had never told her bedtime tales, but Clinton had. "Was it as beautiful as you'd hoped?"

"More so."

Time had been kind to him. He didn't have that many wrinkles, and he had to be about eighty. Gentleness shone from his eyes, and shame hit her in the gut. She'd secretly hated this man because her father had planted his terrible seeds inside her head, yet Clinton hadn't hurt a soul as far as she was aware.

"I'm glad you got to go," she said and found she meant it.

"Me, too, although we paid a price. Sally's poorly. She caught Covid there, and it left behind some nasty surprises. We're hoping she gets better, that the brain fog passes, but I think it's done something else to her. She keeps asking after your mum, seems to forget she died. Maybe you could come and see her."

Faith didn't want this, her past encroaching without her permission. What Clinton had asked was too much. "I…I'm trying to forget…everything."

"You can try, but it'll always follow you. I know you hated me, that you were only being polite to me for your mother."

Unexpected embarrassment poured into her. Faced with this man telling her he'd *known*, yet he'd been nice to her all the same, almost brought her to her knees. He was a better man than any she'd encountered, knowing racism festered in her heart and he'd bought her sweets anyway. Maybe he'd been trying to show her she had nothing to fear, nothing to hate. Maybe he was just good down to his bones, nothing like Dad had painted him to be.

"I'm sorry," she said. "For all of it. I have…I have a grandson. His mother is black."

"I suspect that was tough for you, but it doesn't need to be."

"I know that now. I…"

"Racism is learned, and only you can unlearn it."

She nodded. "I'm trying."

He stood. "Try harder, because your face when you saw me, it said everything. It doesn't have to be like this. You're a decent woman underneath, you just need to let her out." He stood and patted her shoulder. "I'll tell Mrs Whitehall you were nice to me. That's all she wants to know."

He left, taking all of the sunshine in the room with him.

Faith stood there, humiliated, angry, ashamed, guilty, and she shut the door, leaning her forehead on it. Had Lemon ever felt like this, knowing his mother had moulded him like her father had done to her? Had he hated her for it? Was that why he'd gone out with Becky, to show her he wasn't following her doctrine? She'd assumed he'd taken a leaf out of his father's book and had done it to piss her off, to hurt her, but maybe that wasn't the case. Maybe Lemon hadn't seen colour in the way she did.

She changed into her regular clothes, sifting through her emotions. The bottom line was, Dad had been wrong, and it would take a long time for her to unpick the stitches he'd sewn. But a thread already dangled, and it wouldn't take much for her to pull it. Clinton had just shown her what a pure soul he had—perhaps she could have one, too.

She collected her bag, held her head up, and exited her room. She walked towards Petra's desk, her mind on getting home and sorting out her feelings in an attempt to understand her reaction to Clinton when she hadn't known it was him. An immediate aversion. She'd have a rage at her dead father who'd damaged her to such a degree. Admit that Clinton was right, only *she* could unlearn it all. Instead of blaming everyone else, she should take accountability. Educate herself like The Brothers had said. *Finally*, she understood what they'd meant.

She let Petra know she was leaving then headed towards the stairs.

"Faith?"

She stopped, Mrs Whitehall's voice striking the fear of God into her. She turned and smiled, putting on a front, and stared towards her boss' office.

"That wasn't so bad, was it?" Whitehall leaned on the doorframe.

"No, it was fine."

"Watch yourself." Whitehall gave her an eerie smile. "You never know what's around the corner. The mouse needs to be wary of the eagle."

A threat in the form of one of her stupid sayings. Faith managed another smile and nodded. She dashed down the stairs, her legs wobbly, and rushed through the storeroom and into the shop. It stayed open as long as the brothel, and the evening crowd had come in to browse. She ignored the customers and staff, weaving between the stands and out into the street, her chest tight, eyes stinging.

Paranoid now Whitehall had looked into her, had said Faith was a mouse, a *target*, she ran down the street towards the bus stop, desperate to get home where she'd feel safer. If Austin brought the money round later, or even in the morning, she'd fuck off right away, no hanging around to sort out her tenancy or hand in her notice. She could do that when she got to where she was going. She'd get on a train to anywhere and stay in a cheap hotel until she found somewhere to rent. Being on Mrs Whitehall's radar like this wasn't good, and as she stepped onto the bus and swiped her pass card, a thought dumped itself into her head.

What if she was a mouse because of the robbery?

What if it wasn't anything to do with racism?

Mrs Whitehall could be playing with me. That money being back in the safe…that's not right, so something's up.

She wished she'd stolen more, kept it, then she could leave now, she wouldn't have to rely on Austin.

She sat at the back and got her phone out.

FAITH: BRING MY CUT ROUND THIS EVENING. I NEED TO MAKE MYSELF SCARCE.

It took a while for him to answer, so much so that she'd convinced herself again that he'd pissed off with the spoils. He responded just as the bus approached her housing estate.

AUSTIN: OKAY. BE THERE IN AN HOUR.

Relieved, she went through everything in her head. What she should pack. Whether she should let a neighbour know she was going—they could all pick through her house and take what they wanted, she didn't care.

She had to get out of here before the eagle circled then dived down to snatch her up.

Chapter Twenty-One

*F*aith strutted down the street towards home, her demeanour hiding what she really felt inside—she couldn't let Mina know she felt sick and wished tonight had never happened. Difficult, to admit you'd had a hand in killing someone—and that you'd enjoyed it yet at the same time wondered what kind of monster you'd become.

Tarone had died shortly after Ollie had kicked his head for the fifth time, his final breath a wheeze that had ghosted out into the night—everyone had stood so still, their own breaths held as if mimicking Tarone. Then the collective exhale, some nervous laughter, the rumblings of people pretending it had been a job well done, that death, that murder. Except the plan hadn't involved murder, so what happened now? A beating hadn't seemed so bad, but death?

They'd hastily agreed to split up and go home in different directions—a mob would be easier to spot, to remember, and none of them wanted that.

"Bloody hell, what a rush!" Mina looped her arm through Faith's. "I mean, we weren't supposed to kill him—and anyway, Ollie did that, so we're safe as houses, we only kicked him—but who knew doing it would make me feel so alive?"

Faith frowned, glad they were between streetlights so Mina couldn't see her expression. She responded in the way her friend would expect. "Yeah. His fault for nicking stuff."

"Too right. This will send a message—don't mess with us."

It hadn't been about the thefts, though, not really. Any excuse to set upon a black person, that was what Faith had gleaned when Mina had called a meeting *with everyone this morning to explain what was going to happen. None of them seemed that bothered about their trinkets going missing, more that their blood was hot with the need to beat the shit out of Tarone. Faith would like to tell herself their behaviour was gross, but hadn't she got excited herself? Hadn't she looked forward to tonight, counting down the hours so she could see how Dad had felt with Arvinda?*

And what did she feel? Good? Bad?

Both.

It seemed she'd forever be confused about something or other. Never having a clear mind, always asking herself questions about the past, her parents. Now she was older, she looked back on her childhood and knew they were fucked up. The pair of them should never have been together, Mum a punchbag, Dad the boxer, the man who talked so much shit, and so well, so convincingly, he had people believing whatever he said.

He should have been a salesman.

"Do you think we'll get caught?" Faith asked.

Would she live the years ahead the same as her father, wondering when that knock on the door would come? Would she ever admit to anyone, outside of her complicit neighbours, that she'd played a part in Tarone's death? No, she'd be like Mum, keeping it quiet. No way did she want Bailey or Ollie coming after her.

"Nah," Mina said. "For one, he was black, so no one will give a shiny shite he's dead, and two, it was late, most people were in bed, the curtains closed an' all that, and no one was behind us when we followed him — I checked. And now? We've all split up, so…"

Faith had been the first one to draw blood. Even the others who'd kicked Tarone before her hadn't split his lip or busted his nose — they'd kicked his body and the back of his head. Had the sight of that blood in the torchlight riled Ollie up so much he'd kicked and kicked and kicked, wanting Tarone to die?

Mina went on, "We won't even arrive home at the same time, remember? We made sure we'll get back at different times so our other neighbours don't put two and two together when it comes on the news. Which is why we're going to The Club, okay?"

Faith had forgotten about that. It was why she had stilettos on and a nice dress Mina had loaned her. They were off to party at a nightclub, to get seen by as many people as possible.

"My shoes… I've got his blood on them."

"A puddle's up there, look. Give them a wash."

They stopped by the deep water which filled a pothole in the path. Faith stuck the toe of her shoe in, *and a flashback of it hitting Tarone's temple lit up in her mind. Oh God, she'd be sick in a minute if she didn't get a grip. For the first time, she truly understood pack mentality, how none of them were going to back down when so many people had their eyes on each other. The baying for blood was something she'd never encountered before—not like that. There had been punch-ups at school, she'd stood on the peripheral of those, everyone chanting, "Fight, fight, fight!" but that had been different, a few thumps thrown between angry boys and hair-pulling with the girls. This…this was so much more.*

She'd become her father—by choice, willingly—and now walked away from the scene the same as he had, except this time was different as the friends didn't remain behind, they'd all left together, and everyone knew Ollie had killed him. It didn't feel as right as she'd hoped, all this. Maybe she had a bit of Mum in her, where she felt for Tarone, but the problem was, the bit of Dad was so much bigger and overtook everything, just like he'd done in life. He lived and breathed inside her, his voice always there to guide, to convince her she was doing the right thing.

Sometimes, she thought she was going mad when she heard it.

"Come on, let's get pissed," Mina said on a laugh.

Maybe that was for the best. Faith could blot it out, even if only for a while. She'd inspect it all in the morning, see how she felt then.

In The Club, a man came over, said something to Faith, but the music was too loud for her to pick up his words. He jerked his head to the stairs, indicating he wanted her to go up to the quiet area, the seating by the balcony, but she turned away. Why did he seem interested in her? Mum had said she was tainted, so what the hell did he want?

But he doesn't know you're tainted…

Nervous, she moved away, closer to Mina who chatted up some bloke who was three sheets to the wind. His knees kept bobbing, and his eyelids moved up and down slowly, as if he fought staying awake.

Mina swung round to Faith and went close to her ear, shouting, "He's that rat-arsed he won't even get it up. Let's go and find men who aren't drunk."

Mina on the prowl was something Faith had never seen—this was their first time out together. Although Faith had told her and Bailey about Tim, it seemed Mina had forgotten if she thought Faith wanted to find a man to take home. Hurt that she hadn't been considered, that her fear of men didn't matter, she followed her friend through the crowd and pressed her back to the wall while Mina chatted up a blond fella.

She wanted to go home—but not to her bedsit. Oddly, she wanted the comfort of Mum's place. It had never felt like home, not like where she'd lived when Dad had been alive, but it still held a familiarity she craved. Did she want to face Mum, who she'd ignored for months? Did she want to hear her going on and on about Tim and how he'd be coming out of prison soon? Bailey had been keeping an ear out since she'd told them her secret, and before they'd gone out to hurt Tarone, he'd pulled her into the kitchen and shut the door.

"I went down The Eagle at lunchtime. That Tim fella is getting out in a couple of weeks—early because of good behaviour. I know a man, who knows a man, who knows a prison guard, and Tim's not considered a threat to the public now. He's found God or summat—a likely story. Personally, if a bloke preys on a kid, he's always a threat, and I reckon they're only kicking him out because they need his cell—overcrowding, see. But I thought you should know."

Her legs had almost given way. Jesus Christ, Mum would welcome him, he'd move in, get his feet right back under the table. So no, Faith wouldn't go and see

219

her, no matter how much she yearned to be somewhere safe tonight. Her bedsit would never be safe, not now — the police could come at any time if someone had spotted them all. They couldn't be so sure no one had. Couldn't be cocky and complacent.

A geyser of sick erupted in her throat, and she couldn't hold it in. She vomited in the corner, ashamed that people watched her; they'd think she'd drunk too much, but that wasn't anything to do with it.

She wiped her lips with the back of her hand and swigged some of her bottled lager to clean her mouth. She had to get out of here. Everyone seemed too close, too in her face, and the circle around her was a reminder of the one around Tarone. She put her bottle on the floor and pushed between two people, letting Mina know she was going back to the house, and staggered between dancers, out into the fresh air.

She tottered down the street, hugging herself because there was no one else to do it — no one who cared enough to give her a cuddle or even want to.

Clinton would hug you. He cared.

She shuddered at the thought of him putting his arms around her.

Tears stung her eyes. She wasn't exactly a catch, ruined as she was, so she was destined to be alone for the rest of her life. She didn't want a man to touch her—how could she bring herself to stand that? —and the future appeared as a bleak and unhappy one.

"Oi, hold up!"

She glanced over her shoulder. The man from The Club jogged towards her, the one she couldn't hear at the bar. She faced forward and upped her pace, her heart whomping too hard. Why couldn't he just fuck off?

"Hey, you shouldn't be out on your own," he said, coming abreast of her. "I'll walk you home, all right? It isn't safe around here. Someone got murdered earlier."

Her stomach flipped. News had travelled fast. "I don't need walking home."

"All right, if you're worried about me knowing where you live, the house number, I'll just get you to your street."

"You'll still know where I live because you're probably a pervert and will watch where I go."

He laughed. "A pervert? Fuck off!"

She slowed and glanced at him. Dark hair, nice face. He didn't look like a pervert or anyone to worry about, but neither had Tim.

"I'm...I'm not interested," she said. "In you walking me home or whatever else you've got in mind."

"Bloody hell, I was only being a gentleman. My mum would have my guts for garters if I let you go off by yourself."

She relented. "Don't try anything, okay?"

"Like what?"

"Rude stuff."

He laughed again then sobered. "Has someone hurt you? I mean, you're acting well weird."

"Yes, they did. I don't trust men."

"Sorry to hear that. What happened?"

She clamped her lips together. Then blurted, "I was raped at fourteen."

"Fuck me, that's rough."

Why the hell had she told him?

"What's your name?" he asked.

"Faith."

"Let's start again. Hello, Faith, I'm Reggie, and I promise I'm not a rapist."

She chuckled, despite him making light of what had happened to her. "That was a really bad chat-up line."

"I'm full of them. So, what do you do? For work?"

"I'm at the factory."

"Long hours and shit pay, eh?"

"Something like that." Was she supposed to ask what he did? She had no idea.

"I'm a brickie."

"Right."

"I'm going to go solo one day, run my own business."

"Right."

"Be my own boss."

"Right."

"You're not very good at making conversation. What's up with ya?"

She wasn't about to admit that she avoided this sort of thing. "I didn't realise being walked home meant I had to be a Chatty Cathy."

"Blimey, you're a hard nut to crack."

"I don't want to be cracked."

He nudged her arm. "Go on a date with me, and you'll soon thaw out."

She shook her head and ploughed on, wanting to get away from him yet wanting to stay in his company. What the hell was going on?

Chapter Twenty-Two

Austin had checked with the twins as to how he should answer Faith's message—he'd do whatever they asked of him now. He owed them. George had told him to agree to go round there, and he prepared himself to collect Faith's cut from the twins who would be waiting for him at the back of The Angel. He still had to meet up with Benny at seven to trap him, so he was conscious of the time restraints.

He put the empty alcohol bottles in a carrier bag, planning to take them to the recycle bank after he'd seen The Brothers. He drove out of his street, past Entertainment Plaza, the risk-taker in him begging him to stop and visit Jackpot Palace one more time with the last tenner in his wallet. He fought off the urge and continued on, berating himself for ever getting the gambling bug in the first place. He'd known how much it upset Maxine, yet he'd done it anyway, blaming it on her for leaving him.

He needed to take a long hard look at himself and properly admit how much of an arsehole he'd been. He'd ask Vic to help him, do one of those intensive sessions he'd mentioned.

He parked opposite The Angel and walked down the side, past the steel steps and a small white van with some logo or other on the side. His guts churned. What if The Brothers were stringing him along and turned nasty on him, beating the crap out of him round the back? They could drag him inside, into that room he'd confessed everything in, and he doubted that woman behind the desk would breathe a word.

What if they didn't hit him now but used him to lure Benny then finished him off afterwards? They could have found someone else to do the drug drop, not needing him anymore.

He rounded the corner, his knees loosening at the sight of the twins.

"All right?" he asked to test the waters.

"Fucking splendid," George said. "We've been a bit busy."

Greg laughed. "And we're about to get busier."

What did that mean? Austin took one step back, ready to run. Stupid, because they'd catch up with him, and anyway, that bloke who stood in the alley over the road would stop him getting away.

"You look a bit peaky," Greg said.

"I feel sick to be honest. Is this a setup? Are you going to punch me?"

"What?" Greg frowned. "I told you, you're George's project. Stop being a bloody dickhead."

"Sorry."

George stepped forward and whacked a meaty paw on Austin's shoulder. "Calm down. You don't need to go to The Naked Fountain anymore. We've already dealt with Mr Bender.

We paid off the money you owed. You just owe us now, so you'll do the drug drops for free until we're even."

Austin nodded, relieved it was basically over, bar the one remaining worry. "What if Mrs Whitehall's found out about the robbery and gets shitty about what I got Faith to do? What if she does something to me when I go there later?"

"She won't. We've come to an agreement. We deal with you, she deals with Faith—unless she's changed her mind on that and hasn't told us. You've got the better end of the bargain."

That meant Faith was going to die. All because of him.

"Thanks. I mean it. I'll do whatever you want, I swear."

"Just deliver this to Faith for now." George handed over a thick envelope. "Whitehall wants her to take the cash. Probably another one of her sick games, or maybe she wants proof Faith isn't to be trusted. I suspect someone will be there, watching the handover, so be careful."

Austin's guts burned, sour acid swirling. "Fuck."

"We'll be there an' all. When you get there, wait for either of us to give you the nod as to when you hand her the money. We'll also follow you to Whitehall's later."

"Cheers." Austin had to know. "What did you do to Benny?"

"Shot him in the head. And if those two blokes of his show up at yours again, let us know straight away. Then *they'll* get a bullet in the head. Right, off you go."

Austin jogged back to his car and got in, putting the envelope on the passenger seat. About to switch on the engine, he changed his mind and, while the twins got into the white van, he checked the envelope's contents, just in case he *was* being set up. About five grand stared back at him, and he removed one of the notes. Taking the rest of the stash from the robbery out of the glove box—he hadn't got rid of it yet like George had told him to—he compared a fake note to the real one. They appeared the same, felt the same, so whoever had made the counterfeit lot was a bloody good forger.

He could maybe get away with spending the fakes somewhere; it seemed a shame, a waste to ditch it. But what if the twins asked for it and he'd already spent it all? He glanced out of the window and waited for George to reverse so their vehicles sat side by side. Austin lowered the window and held the money bag out. A pang of greed almost had him swiping it back inside, but no, he had to be on the level now he was under their thumb, couldn't risk fucking about.

Greg's window sailed down, and his hand stretched out to take the bag.

"The shit left over from the robbery," Austin said. "I don't trust myself not to get rid of it."

Greg nodded, and the van peeled away.

An odd sense of a weight being lifted came over Austin. It wasn't so bad to do the right thing after all, and once he'd paid the twins back, maybe they'd pay him for the drops after that, or other jobs, and he wouldn't be skint anymore. Mind you, now he didn't owe Benny, he had five hundred a month spare, so life wasn't so bad.

He pulled away from the kerb, heading for Faith's. He felt bad for her. She'd only nicked the money because he'd forced her to, and in her message she'd said she needed to make herself scarce. Did that mean she was aware Mrs Whitehall knew what she'd done? Whatever, it wasn't Austin's business. He was playing the part The Brothers wanted him to, and he wouldn't deviate.

He coasted down her street slowly, looking into parked cars for anyone watching. Some bearded bloke in a beanie hat and a boiler suit tinkered under the bonnet of his Mercedes up ahead, a car that stood out in these parts—too posh for the likes of the residents. He had to be Mrs Whitehall's fella, didn't he? The one who wanted proof of the money changing hands. Nervous, Austin slid his car into a spot two doors down from Faith's and contemplated whether to get out or not—would it be better if he stayed in the car and got her to come outside? At least then he wasn't a sitting duck if he stood at her front door.

The white van went past, putting his mind at rest; it stopped beside the big fella, and George lowered the window and spoke to him. Then the van moved off to park in a space one house up.

GG: Bloke's aware we're watching. Go and give her the money.

Austin: I'm going to ask her to come out. I don't trust that bloke.

Austin switched over to Faith's message thread.

Austin: I'm outside in my car. Come and collect.

FAITH: NO, THERE'S A MAN OUT THERE, HAVEN'T SEEN HIM BEFORE. SOMEONE IN A VAN JUST SPOKE TO HIM THEN PARKED UP. IT'S IFFY.

AUSTIN: YOU'RE PARANOID.

FAITH: JUST PUT IT THROUGH THE LETTERBOX.

As Mrs Whitehall wanted photos, Austin had to ensure Faith came into view.

AUSTIN: JESUS, I'LL COME TO THE DOOR, ALL RIGHT? IF HE'S DODGY, HE'LL HAVE TO GET PAST ME FIRST.

Not that Austin could do anything, fucking wet lettuce that he was, but Faith thought he was someone to be wary of. He messaged the twins to let them know the change of plan, then got out, hoping to God they had guns trained on Mercedes Man in case he had one of his own and let a bullet fly. It would be sod's law for Austin to die now, when he'd got everything but the drug drop sorted, his life heading in the right direction at last.

He knocked on her door, not daring to turn around to give Mercedes Man a clear shot at his face—with a gun or a camera. He took one step to the side so any photos would include Faith clearly—and he felt a wanker for it, but what else could he do? He had new rules to follow. Maxine would be so ashamed of him if she knew what he was up to.

The door opened, and Faith's face appeared in the narrow gap. "Give it to me."

"Why are you hiding like that?"

"I told you, that man." She stared over Austin's shoulder.

"He's just fixing his fucking car!"

"So he'd have us believe. Look, hand the money over and piss off. I've got things to do."

"Like what?"

"I'm getting out of here."

Austin pushed the door, Faith blocking it from going further.

"Listen to me, you stupid bitch. I warned you I'd strangle you, so do what I say, else I'll make good on my threat. Open that fucking door a bit and then you can have the money."

Faith darted her gaze out into the street. "Are you setting me up?"

"No, just do what I asked, then I'll fuck off. You'll never see me again."

"Why do I need to open the door more, then?"

Austin didn't have a good enough answer without putting himself in the shit—he couldn't exactly say Mrs Whitehall wanted a picture of the money changing hands. He stepped back a couple of paces and dropped the envelope on the pavement, far enough away that she'd have to leave her house to get it. Another few steps, and he stood on the road between the bumpers of two parked cars. Faith glared at him, then at the envelope. She lunged into the street, snatched it up, and retreated inside, slamming the door shut.

He turned to go back to his car.

"Perfect," Mercedes Man said. "Cheers for that."

Austin let out a long breath, feeling a right bastard for what he'd done. But it was a game of survival, and he didn't intend to be on Mrs Whitehall's radar. He got in the car and drove into the next street, parking up again.

AUSTIN: CAN I GO HOME AND GET SOME GRUB NOW?

GG: GO TO THE NOODLE AND TIGER. WE'LL MEET YOU THERE.

Now, more than ever, he knew what it was like to be someone's bitch.

Better than being dead, though.

He drove away, thinking of the empty bottles he was supposed to dump, worrying about Faith and what her fate would be. He'd played a part in sealing it, and he could only hope her death was quick and painless.

Although he doubted it would be.

Chapter Twenty-Three

Faith had got her possessions down to one large suitcase. Everything else she wished she could take were nostalgic items, sentimental things she didn't have a use for but loved having around her just the same. Lemon's first drawing from playgroup that had been taped to her fridge inside a plastic sleeve so it didn't get ruined. She couldn't bear to part with that so had packed it, but the rest...she had to let go. She'd taken pictures so she still had a reminder, and that would have to do. Just because they wouldn't be to hand, didn't mean she had to forget them.

Austin had acted so strangely, ensuring she came out onto the path to get the money. At the point she'd snatched the envelope up, she'd taken a quick glance over the road, and the man by the Mercedes had held his phone up, his thumb tapping away as if he took several pictures. She'd shit herself and dashed inside, sitting on the stairs, her mind a mess. She'd had the hideous sense of being trapped indoors, in a place where she should feel safe, an animal in her cage, the people outside wishing her ill-will. At least Austin hadn't barged his way in and strangled her.

She'd counted the money—five grand, easily enough to get her a cheap place up north, away from the ridiculous London prices. She'd looked out of the living room window, keeping out of the way so she wouldn't be seen, and the man fixing his car was still there, but he no longer had his head under the bonnet. He sat in the driver's seat reading a newspaper. The van had gone just after Austin, and Faith had the awful sense he was going to be accosted somewhere, that Mrs Whitehall knew everything and she was rounding the pair of them up.

Faith would have to leave via the back way.

Now, she went upstairs to stare down at her garden and the alley behind it, checking for another man lurking. No one was out there bar Mr Sneddon, the old man she'd barked at last week because he'd had a go at her for filling her recycle bin so much the lid hadn't closed and flies were everywhere. Should she open the window and call out for help? Would he even want to give her the time of day, considering the way she'd always treated him as a pest, no one she was interested in? She couldn't blame him if he ignored her. *She* wouldn't help her if she was someone else. She'd tell her she was on her own.

On the bus home from work, she'd changed her mind and opted not to let anyone around here know she was leaving London. She'd phone her landlord next week and tell him she no longer wanted to live here. She was supposed to give a month's notice, but he could go and fuck himself—he'd never been quick at doing any repairs, and the bathroom still had damp in the top corner, something he was supposed to have sorted months ago. Why should she do the right thing by him when he hadn't for her?

She'd already deleted the rent standing order from her banking app, so if he thought he was getting more money out of her, he could think again. Besides, he could keep the bond, so sod him.

She checked herself. Back to being moody, bitchy Faith. Was it any wonder, though, that she'd reverted to who she'd been for years, the spiteful-woman persona a comfort blanket, familiar, when the new one she hoped to be was so alien? She didn't know how to cope as her, not yet.

She took one last look around each room upstairs, pausing in Lemon's bedroom doorway. The police had been to collect some of his things, evidence for God knew what, and they hadn't returned them. She supposed she ought to tell them her new address when she finally settled, they'd need to let her know when Lemon's body was being released, but she'd deal with that when the time came. She'd arrange for a cremation and the ashes to be sent to wherever she ended up. Forgoing his funeral wasn't something she'd ever imagined doing, but Mrs Whitehall would go, expecting to catch Faith there, and it would all be over.

For now, she had to concentrate on her escape.

Downstairs, she glanced around and discovered that leaving wasn't the wrench she'd thought it would be since she'd done her mourning while packing. This house, full of things that reminded her of Reggie, the wallpaper the same as the day he'd walked out, the carpets unchanged, was a ball and chain around her neck. She should have moved out after he had so the memories didn't linger, but of course, her excuse had been that she didn't want to uproot Lemon, when in fact, she'd remained for selfish reasons. She was one of the queen bees around here, and to lose that, to start up elsewhere, struggling to climb the social ladder again, had scared her silly. It had been so important, her status, something she'd fought for, to be noticed, listened to, feared, because God knew she'd been ignored enough as a child, her parents too intent on arguing to really be bothered with her.

Was that true? Or was she skewing the narrative again? Was she remembering things how she wanted to remember them rather than face the fact that apart from Dad yammering on about people who didn't belong, and her listening to their rows, it hadn't been *that* bad?

How times had changed. She couldn't *wait* to be an unknown now. Couldn't wait to be as invisible as she'd started to become here. No one would know her past, no one could guess at her shame, and no one would be aware of who she'd married and how she'd behaved. Who her son had been. An assassin.

She sank into an armchair, thinking it best to leave when it got dark. Less eyes on her walking off, then. If she could get away with escaping unnoticed, it would be days before her neighbours twigged, and by then, she'd be long gone, perhaps ensconced in a little cottage by the sea somewhere if she was lucky. Whoever that man was out the front had a long wait, because he wouldn't be seeing her again.

She closed her eyes, conjuring up a turquoise sea and a white sandy beach. Clinton strolled on the sand, but the younger man he'd been in her childhood, not the one he'd aged into. How kind of him to come today, although she was under no illusion he'd been forced into it by Mrs Whitehall or her men, but in his gentle way, regardless of how she'd felt about him, he'd still let her know that he'd been asked to observe her behaviour towards him and would report back to her boss that she'd been nice.

Despite it all, he hadn't wanted to get her in trouble, he'd warned her.

And there she'd been, refusing his request to go and see Sally.

I'm such a cow.

Maybe a leopard couldn't change its spots after all, no matter how much it tried.

She deserved everything Mrs Whitehall wanted to throw at her, but she wasn't about to stick around and take her punishment, because *she* also deserved a second chance, to be who she *should* have been, an innocent person who'd never done anyone wrong. Dad had snatched that way from her, and she'd allowed it to continue after his death. But no more foisting the sole blame onto him, she had to take accountability for herself and also for what Reggie had turned her into. She could have run away from him several times but hadn't.

She drifted off, telling herself to carry her suitcase to the end of the back alley because the wheels turning on the path would get people to their rear windows. A moonlight flit of sorts, a thief in the night, skittering away in shame.

That feeling was back again, the one she'd had when she'd discovered Tim in her bedroom. In the semi-darkness, someone else breathed, their shape close but not too close, far enough away that she made out their whole body. A big body. Wide.

A man, then. And she wasn't as scared this time. She wasn't fourteen. She had years of abuse under her belt and a strong will to survive, so unless he shot her, incapacitated her, she'd put up a fight.

She glanced at the green illuminated numbers of the clock over the mantel.

She'd slept for ages.

"I wondered when you were going to stop snoring," he said.

She recognised the voice and should have known it would be him Mrs Whitehall sent. Despite her mouth going dry and her heart rate scattering now she knew exactly who she was dealing with, she thought back to the man under the bonnet. Bungle with a beard and glasses, the beanie hat covering his hair, the boilersuit obscuring his usual suit and the tie pin showing the word SECURITY.

"What do you want?" she managed.

"You've been a naughty girl, and I've come to do what the boss wants."

Oh God, she'd been so close to leaving, being free. Why had she decided to stay until night fell? Why hadn't she just fucked off as soon as Austin had been round? What did it *matter* if anyone saw her leaving? Why did she think she always knew best?

Because the man—*Bungle*—had been out the front and she'd thought she was safe to have a nap, to wait, that he was only keeping an eye on her. That Mrs Whitehall was playing the long game, waiting it out, seeing how Faith reacted tomorrow at work when *still* no one mentioned the theft.

I'm such a stupid, stupid bitch.

"I haven't done anything," she said, prepared to maintain her innocence, to fight for her freedom. If she could just get him to believe her, put doubt in his head, she had a chance.

"Oh, I think you have." He moved his arm, and a rectangle of light lit up his features, showcasing his fake beard, the phone screen reflected in his glasses lenses. He held it close to his face and pressed the screen a few times. Then he turned it around, stalked nearer, until the mobile was about a metre away.

On it, she stuffed money into the bag, and she didn't need to watch anymore to know the whole robbery had been filmed. She thought to where the camera must be, above the clock on the right-hand wall, maybe even inside it, and all this time she'd thought there wasn't any CCTV. How naïve of her, how utterly dumb.

The footage had been edited and spliced, switching to her leaving Len's office and going downstairs. Through the storeroom with the black sack. Putting the sack in the bin. Going back indoors. Then came video of her in her room, and seeing herself with the punters, having *sex*, brought on tears and rage and embarrassment and hatred for herself at having to do that to make a living. This was a violation of her privacy, of the clients' privacy, but it wasn't like she could complain, was it? She'd been caught bang to rights, and there was no talking her way out of this.

She had to get away from Bungle. So long as she could take her handbag with the money, her passport, and birth certificate in it, she didn't care about the suitcase.

"There's another one," he said. "Might explain a few things for you." He jabbed at the screen again then showed her the phone.

Satin, taking photos of the money in the safe. She removed it, putting it into a briefcase, then opened a holdall and placed more money in the safe. She referred to the pictures she'd taken, switching some piles around, making sure they matched, then she closed the safe, picked up the holdall and briefcase, and left the office. The scene switched to her opening the safe again, except it was empty this time, and she put the money from the briefcase inside.

"The cash you stole was counterfeit," he said, as if she needed an explanation. "Apart from Mike's money, of course."

She thought of the envelope Austin had given her. Shit, would she get away with spending fake notes? Would she get caught, arrested? She'd have to hope she got away with using it, because she needed to pay a new landlord.

A plan of action formed.

"Am I allowed to make a cuppa?" she asked.

He slid the phone in his pocket. "I've got a machete, so any hassle…"

"I'll behave."

"Mine's a coffee, two sugars and milk."

She rose on shaky legs, feeling her way out of the murky living room and down the hallway. Would he follow her? Trust that she wouldn't leave via the back door and leg it through the garden? Or were others here now, out the front *and* the back, waiting for her to do that?

She turned the kitchen light on, unsettled that the blinds were down on the window and door, that he'd come in here and done that. Had he been upstairs, too? How had he got in without her hearing him? A lock pick? It must have been, as no pieces of glass littered the floor where he might have smashed a window, unless he'd snooped for her dustpan and brush and cleaned it up. God, she must have been right out for the count.

At the sink, she filled the kettle to maximum and put it on its base, flicking the switch. With the blind down, she couldn't see his reflection in the glass to know if he'd followed her, but she sensed him, the air charged with his presence. She went about as if it were perfectly normal to have an uninvited man with a machete in her house, taking the milk from the fridge then collecting two cups like it didn't matter. She took a packet of Super Noodles from the top cupboard and held it up, her back to him.

"Do you want any?"

"Can do. Haven't eaten since lunchtime."

How creepy that he could speak so calmly, as though he wasn't going to cart her back to the brothel and let Mrs Whitehall do whatever the hell she liked. She'd thought Bungle liked her, maybe fancied her, and to realise his loyalty was firmly in Whitehall's camp let her know she wasn't important—again—and her feelings hadn't been taken into consideration and likely never would be. Bungle would go where the pay was, and that certainly wasn't with her.

She picked out another packet of noodles and removed a saucepan from a lower cupboard, placing it on the hob and emptying the noodles into it. She had plans for that. The kettle clicked off, so she filled the cups then the saucepan and lit the gas underneath. Busying herself with the tea and coffee kept her focused on what she'd do to him, how she'd get away. It was a case of survival, would be an act of self-defence. Once she'd floored the bastard, ensured he was out cold, she'd go cap in hand to The Brothers and ask them for help in getting her somewhere safe. Beg for a loan in case Austin's money was fake. She wasn't brave enough to do this on her own, not with Mrs Whitehall being involved.

Good job she was leaving the car behind, because it might well have a tracker on it. She should have sold it long ago as she'd always found getting the bus to work easier.

What if the twins tell me to get fucked?

They would at first, but she'd remind them she was a resident and they had a promise to uphold—to help anyone who asked. She almost laughed at that. Who the fuck did she think she was, *expecting* them to be kind to her? That promise didn't extend to her.

She put Bungle's coffee on the worktop to her right and sipped her tea, the noodle water bubbling to her left. She'd used a weighty pan on purpose, one she could swing, and with the bottom being so hot, she'd hopefully burn the fuck out of his face.

At last, she turned round to lean her backside on the sink unit, keeping him in her peripheral. He drank his coffee. Where was the machete? In the living room? Or had he lied and come in unarmed? He pulled his phone out and casually browsed. It was now or never, the perfect chance to belt him with the pan while he was distracted. Slowly, she inched towards the cooker, doing it carefully and in small increments so he didn't notice she moved away. She placed her cup down and checked what he was doing—laughing at something on his screen. Was it at a video of her, in her work room, being used by clients?

She grabbed the pan and swung out round, catching him on the back of the head, cursing herself for missing his face completely. He bent over, an "Oof!" gusting out of him. Noodles went flying through the air to land in the sink, draping over the taps, the water slapping surfaces. Faith stared at him holding the back of his head, his phone falling to the floor.

She got a shift on and ran out. Closed the kitchen door to buy some time, snatching her handbag off the bottom stair and wrenching the front door open. On her way up the street, small stones digging into her bare feet, she fished in her bag and took her phone out, glancing back to see if he'd followed her.

No sign of him.

She pushed on, fumbling with the lock screen code and failing on the first attempt. On the second go, she managed it, crying out in relief, and found the message string she'd had with Laura Gardiner from number one a few weeks back when Faith had been purging some of her clothes, Laura taking them off her hands. She ran faster, needing somewhere to stop so she could text her, dipping into an alley between houses.

FAITH: GET HOLD OF THE BROTHERS SOMEHOW. TELL THEM MRS WHITEHALL SENT BUNGLE ROUND. I NEED TO SEE THEM. IN DANGER. QUICKLY! I'LL WAIT ROUND THE BACK OF MY HOUSE IN SNEDDON'S GARDEN.

She stuffed her phone in her bag and poked her head out of the alley.

Bungle stood *right there*, grinning down at her. He didn't have his boilersuit on anymore, appearing incongruous in her street in his security uniform, having no authority here but looking like he did.

He sniffed as though the smell of her repulsed him. "You hurt my fucking head."

She stepped back, ready to dash down the alley. She'd made a mistake, should have hammered on someone's door or phoned the police while she'd been running down the street.

He gripped the front of her top and hauled her towards him. She bashed into him. She opened her mouth to scream, but he clamped his free hand over it, spun her round so her back was to his chest, and lifted her feet off the ground. He marched along the street. She kicked and fought, but he held her fast.

"Pack it the fuck in, you daft mare."

Faith dropped her bag, needing someone, anyone, to find it and realise something was wrong. He took her inside, shut the door, and hoisted her into the kitchen, where he sat her on a chair.

Hand still over her mouth, the other gripping the back of her hair, he leaned down to whisper, "I don't like people who hurt my head."

He sounded simple, something she'd never picked up on before, but despite that, he didn't seem in the mood to listen to anything she had to say. She stared at the saucepan on the floor, her only weapon, as it appeared he'd taken her knife block away. Why hadn't she noticed that before? What the fuck was *wrong* with her?

He sniffed her again. "There was this kid at school once, *he* hurt my head. Do you know what I did to him?"

Faith couldn't answer, so she shook her head.

He grinned. "I bit his fucking ear off."

Faith's legs shook, bouncing up and down, and she reached up to scratch his face, seeing as his hands were occupied. But his arms were in the way, her move ineffectual.

He sighed. "You're really grinding my gears, woman."

He took his hand from her mouth then punched it. Pain speared into her gums and lips, a tooth coming loose, blood flooding her tongue. Her eyes watered, and she blinked to clear them. He studied her, a strange expression morphing his features, and he resembled someone who detested her. Had she looked at Clinton like that? Had *her* hatred been so obvious?

Bungle hefted her up high then threw her to the floor. Her arse landed on noodle water, agony shooting into her coccyx and up her spine. She scrabbled to get up, slipping all over the place, desperation sending her into a panic. She grabbed the saucepan and managed to get to her feet. Too late, though. He was at her, hands clamping on her shoulders, pushing her backwards against the larder cupboard door. A hand clamped around her throat and squeezed. She'd been in this situation before, except it had been Reggie standing in Bungle's place, Reggie who'd made her feel like a useless slag, on the rubbish heap, used and washed-up, ugly.

Anger surged, and she kneed Bungle in the bollocks. He glared down at her, his face going red, and coughed, his eyes streaming, his hold on her neck getting tighter.

"You shouldn't have done that. Another woman did that to me once. Do you know what I did to her?"

Oh God, he was insane.

"I sliced her nipples off."

Was he telling her that was her fate? A bitten ear and hacked-off nipples? What if she hurt him another way, would he claim someone else had done that, too? Had it really happened, or was he toying with her to increase her fear?

She struggled for air, her lungs burning.

"One for the road, eh?"

He eased up on her throat and wrenched her leggings and knickers to her thighs. Shoved his hand between her legs. Memories of Tim crashed in, and she fought against Bungle, doing what she should have done as a teenager and battled a man who wanted what wasn't his to take. Bungle's strength was too much for her, and a crack of his fist to the side of her head sent her opposing temple smashing into the wall. Pain flourished and grew. He yanked her leggings and knickers right down, past her knees, copping another feel. Bile rose into the back of her mouth. She hawked and spat it at him, the glob landing on his cheek, but it had no effect. He grinned at her, the flames of the Hell entering his eyes.

"Did someone else spit at you once?" she jeered. "Are you going to tell me what you did to *them* an' all?"

"No, I'm going to show you."

He tossed her to the floor again. Pulled something out of his pocket. A condom. He'd *planned* to do this? He fumbled to put it on. Took her. She closed her eyes and cleared her mind, refusing to acknowledge what he was doing; at least she'd have the satisfaction of not suffering the way he likely wanted her to if she was off elsewhere, in another world.

At least she'd have her dignity this time.

Bungle had watched Faith many a time on the security cameras, and while she was an older bird, he'd fancied her something rotten for a while. A shame, then, that the boss wanted her dead, whatever way Bungle chose, but before she died, he'd finally got to fuck her. He'd never look a gift horse in the mouth.

He got up, tucked himself away, and zipped up his trousers. Stared down at her inert form. She cried, but silently, as if sobbing would show her weakness, something she wouldn't want. She'd always had a mouth on her, a snippy tongue, so to see her like this came as a surprise. He'd bargained on her flaming spirit, her taunting him that he had a small dick, anything to rile him up. Instead, she'd gone inside herself like that other woman he'd raped.

He opened the larder door and took the machete out. Glanced at her and held it up. Her eyes widened, the fear of death infiltrating them, but he ignored it—no time for sentimentality here, the 'what could have been' if he'd asked her out on a date previous to this. She shouldn't have stolen from the boss, and what he planned to dish out to her, she deserved. He moved to her side and raised the machete. Brought it down on her neck, all his force behind it.

The blade sliced through cleanly, embedding in the floor, and he had to give it a bit of a tug to lift it. Her face rolled to one side, the neck stump pissing blood, the open slice on her body pumping out the claret. The scarlet puddle spread, a living entity, covering the lino, and he waited for it to slow. It seemed every pint had oozed out. It crept towards him, so he stepped away, back to the larder, and took out his galoshes he'd hidden there. Slid his feet into them. Put on his fisherman's waterproof jacket and gloves.

Things were about to get messy.

India laughed at the pictures Bungle had sent. What a delightful man, one who didn't shy away from the filthy grunt work. He'd receive a good bonus for this.

He was on his way to dispose of the fisherman's clothing, his boilersuit, and the work suit he'd had on underneath. His shoes. The machete. Nothing of him would be left behind or kept, not even the black sack he'd ripped from a roll under the kitchen sink, which he'd used to transport the bloodied clothing to the Mercedes.

That vehicle would also be disposed of.

A job well done. She only wished she'd been there to witness it in person.

Chapter Twenty-Four

*"*W*hat the fuck are you doing home so early?"* Reggie barked. *"Jesus, if you're going to go for only an hour or two, you won't earn enough. I told you, four hours or more. There's a nifty suit I've got my eye on, and I need the cash."*

"I've been raped," she said.

She held her breath, waiting for a kind response, the same one she'd received from the policeman on the desk all those years ago. The one she'd never had from her mother who now pretended the violation hadn't happened.

"Not surprising," Reggie said, sprawled on the sofa, his hairy gut poking out from the bottom of his white T-shirt, one she'd washed and ironed because he never lifted a finger to help. All he did was spend her earnings, order her about, and hit her if she didn't do what he wanted. "The job you do, it's not exactly a shock, is it? What did you expect? Anyway, I don't like you coming home before midnight."

"Why not?"

"None of your fucking business!" He turned to her, a glare of hatred sent her way. "Don't you question me, woman. Ever."

It had been a test, her telling him, to see whether he detested her as much as she thought. It seemed he did, because there wasn't an ounce of sympathy in his words or expression. All he was bothered about was how it affected him.

He'd changed so much since that first night at The Club. At least he'd been nice then. The years since they'd met had coalesced into a chunk of time she could never get back. She should have trusted her instincts back then and insisted she walked home by herself. He'd wheedled his way into her affections, though, made her believe being with a man would be the best thing for her, and now look. He was Dad all over again, convincing her with his words until she believed whatever he wanted her to.

What did he need a suit for? Why didn't he want her coming home early? Was he playing away? Who was it, one of the neighbours? He'd always fancied Jackie, that much was obvious, but would she want anything to do with him? Did she fancy him back?

Do I even care?

And who was he these days? She didn't know him anymore. Wished she'd never known him. Wished she hadn't glanced back when he'd called out to her when she'd left The Club. But then she wouldn't have had Little Lemon, and she'd never regret that. That boy was her life, and she'd teach him like Dad had taught her, to stand up for himself against people who didn't belong. Maybe that should include his father, too. That man didn't belong here, influencing them, but she was too afraid to kick him out.

Reggie shoved a finger up his nose and had a good old dig, his attention on the telly. God, she hated him. She should have stayed single.

"So if he raped you," he said, "he didn't pay you, is that what you're saying?"

"Yes."

"Then you're short on cash. Get back out there and sort another few punters."

She should have known that was what he'd say; he had no compassion. She sighed inwardly so as not to make a noise. She didn't dare give him something else to have a go at her about. With their son tucked up in bed before she'd left to go to 'work', she had no excuse not to go back out there. The housework was up to date, all the washing done. And it wasn't like she'd love a night in front of the telly, was it…

Chance would be a fine thing.

She left the house, walking to the bus stop that would take her to a patch away from the neighbours and Cardigan. She couldn't risk being seen, couldn't handle the disgust and ridicule they'd throw her way. Her job had to be kept a secret. Besides, if Reggie found out someone had seen her, he'd get angry and take it out on her.

She reached the bus stop and sat under the awning. He'd been nice at first, Reggie, buying her small presents and paying for her drinks when they'd gone to the pub on dates. It had lasted two years, that persona, her none the wiser that underneath lurked an arsehole. He'd switched after she'd married him and had given birth to Lemon, said she ought to get back to work and bring some money in, that she'd been lazy for long enough.

Lazy? Caring for their baby had been a full-time job.

Faith had done as she'd been told. Reggie spoke to her the way Dad had spoken to Mum, so it seemed normal to her. A neighbour had looked after Lemon as she was at home all day now and on disability, her back giving her hassle.

Going back to the factory hadn't been so bad, the job a bit monotonous, and Faith had yawned a lot, but it meant she'd had a pay packet to hand over to Reggie at the end of the week, something to make him happy.

He'd taken to drinking more after that, telling her she was boring to be around in the evenings, so he'd gone off to the pub, leaving her knackered from the factory and still having to deal with Lemon. She'd bought their son a pale-yellow teddy last week out of the Child Benefit, and he took it to bed each night, cuddling it something silly. Reggie hadn't been best pleased, saying it was a waste of money and their boy would grow up gay if he played with the bear.

He's bloody ridiculous.

She got on the bus, sore between her legs, her jaw aching from where the rapist had punched her. She'd contemplated going to the police like she had as a teen but talked herself out of it. All the tests, the questions…no, and in her profession, like Reggie had said, it was to be expected.

She sat and stared out of the window at the dark city as it sped by, the chuntering bus taking her to The Moon Estate where she'd stand in her usual spot and pretend she liked shagging men for money. The thought of it had her feeling sick, and she blinked back tears.

Why was life so difficult? It seemed it always had been ever since she could remember. Confusion and anxiety had followed her from childhood, and she laughed to herself at how stupid she'd been, thinking Reggie had saved the day when she'd met him. Getting married and having a baby had given her the brief illusion she'd have a happy life going forward, but how quickly that had shifted into the nightmare she now lived.

Her foray into prostitution had come one night a few months ago, Reggie pissed as a fart, staggering in from the pub and saying some woman had propositioned him, quoting her price. It had got him thinking, and if Faith serviced five men a night, they'd be loaded.

"What?" she'd said. "Are you suggesting what I think you are?"

He'd clamped a hand around her throat, pushing her against the larder door and breathing his foul alcohol fumes in her face. "You're going to do it whether you like it or not, do you understand? Saves your old dear looking after our Lemon. I don't like what she's teaching him, all that having manners business and telling him to mind them. If he doesn't want to say please and thank you, he doesn't have to, just like me."

Faith had struggled to draw air into her lungs, his grip getting tighter. "I'll do it, I'll do it."

She couldn't believe she'd agreed to having men pawing her.

It had meant leaving her friends at the factory — although she couldn't really call them friends. She'd let out her frustrations about her home life at work, barking at people and generally being a snide cow, jealous of them and their perfect husbands. She'd gained the reputation of being a spiteful bitch, so not going there had been for the best, hadn't it?

A streak of light from a lamppost brought her back to the present, and she sighed, wishing she could be anywhere but here, be someone else. The Faith she'd become wasn't someone she'd want to know. Just this morning she'd shouted at Carol down the road, calling her a slag for kicking her husband out and moving another bloke in straight away—something Faith wished she could do. It seemed everyone else had what she wanted, and she was being left behind, handed a raw deal.

The women of the street only tolerated her, that much was clear—she'd made a name for herself as someone to be feared, her only foothold in a world where deep inside, she floundered. She didn't have anyone she could go and tell her secrets to, to ask for help when it came to Reggie—Mina had moved up north, and Bailey had died. Half of the people she knew thought it was a woman's lot to get walloped by her fella, and the other half reckoned if you didn't like the heat, get out of the bloody kitchen.

It wasn't as simple as that. Reggie had threatened her with death if she ever thought of leaving him, and she believed him. He, however, could leave her whenever he wanted, so he'd said, and she wouldn't have a say in that.

She hoped he would.

The bus hissed to a stop, and she got off, walking to her spot around the corner down the lane. Several other sex workers stood there, most of them ravaged by drugs, their prettiness wrecked from the heroin they forced into their veins, teeth on the cusp of turning black, their lips cracked and dry. Maybe that was why

Faith got so many customers—she didn't look half dead.

"Where did you get off to?" Diamond asked.

God knew what her real name was, and Faith didn't much care.

"I nipped home." She wouldn't say why.

The others had been raped at various times, and they'd cried and spoken about it in depth afterwards, everyone crowding round to offer their sympathies, not to mention a few choice words regarding what they'd like to do to the men who'd done it. But they didn't have the guts, didn't even want to go to the police who'd shrug off their claims and be like Reggie, saying, "What did you expect?" During those times, Faith had pretended she couldn't hear their sorry tales, not wanting to be drawn in, because if she was, she might have opened her mouth and told them about Tim, caught in a weak moment like she'd been with Bailey and Mina.

"What for?" Diamond stuck a lock of hair in her mouth and sucked the end.

"You'll grow a hair tree in your stomach if you keep doing that." Faith winced. Her mother's words had come out. God.

"So they say. Your last punter came back about half an hour ago, wanted to know where you were."

Faith froze. The rapist. Why *had he come back? For another go? He'd dropped her off down the far end of the lane afterwards, her stupidly thinking he'd still pay her. Instead, when she'd opened the passenger door, he'd pushed her out onto the road, driving off with her feet still in the footwell, the bottom of the open door catching her temple.*

She raised a hand to rub it. "Watch him, he's not safe."

Diamond inched closer. "Shit, is that why you went home? Did he rip you down there or summat and you needed a sanitary pad? You could have asked me for one of those."

"No!"

Diamond shrugged. "Blimey, I only offered. Keep your hair on. So did he hurt you?"

"Don't go near him. He doesn't pay. Tell the others."

Kenise sashayed over, just starting her shift. She never stood with the junkies, so it was a surprise she'd come anywhere near Diamond. "Tell the others what?"

Faith couldn't stand her and stepped away.

Diamond took her hair out of her mouth. "That the bloke in the white Ford, the one with the well bushy eyebrows who likes rough play, he didn't pay her."

270

Kenise tutted. "I haven't been with him yet."

Faith opened her mouth before she could stop herself. "He doesn't like blacks, that's why."

Kenise raised her eyebrows. "Someone *you* should get along with, then."

Faith turned her back and stared down the lane, hoping a punter came along so she wouldn't have to breathe the same air as her.

"No point being high and mighty with me," Kenise said. "I know your husband pretty well. I'd say if he's coming to me, then you're not giving him what he needs. He hasn't got a problem with my skin."

Faith spun round, anger barging through her that this…this cow had spoken to her like that. "What did you say?"

"I've fucked him. He even gives me a tip, bitch." Kenise smirked. "What, you don't like getting insults thrown at you? Welcome to the fucking club, darling." She stepped forward. Glared. "I don't take shit from anyone, d'you get me? I kept my mouth shut about your old man because I felt sorry for you, but you just crossed a line. Now, I wouldn't piss on you if you were on fire."

She swanned away to stand beneath a streetlight. Faith stared at her back, wanting to launch herself at

her and punch her smug face, but the hurt inside her,
the embarrassment, pinned her to the pavement.

Reggie was shagging her? A black *woman?*

What he'd said made sense now, about her not
coming home early. And he'd done it with Kenise on
purpose. Had he come here when Faith wasn't working
and picked Kenise up, probably laughing because he
knew her aversion, how much it affected her? He
wanted to spite her for not being whatever the fuck he
wanted her to be.

"Jesus, I wouldn't get on the wrong side of her,"
Diamond muttered.

Faith rounded on her. "Oh, just fuck off, you skanky
little slag. Go and take an overdose and do the world a
favour." She stalked off, storming past Kenise to the
next streetlight along—that way, she'd get to the
customers before her, before any of the dirty slappers.

But you're one of them, so you're dirty, too…

She blinked back the burn of tears and stuck a smile
on at the approach of a car, its headlights round, not
square like the rapist's, so she was safe. She cleared her
mind of everything, coaching herself to get through a
few more punters and not tell Reggie how many she'd
had—she'd keep half the money, tell him it had been a
slow night. She'd save so she could escape with Lemon.
Reggie likely used her earnings to pay Kenise, and that

stung, so she was only taking it back. How many times had he been with her, though?

The client slowed, stared at her through the driver's-side window, then sped up and stopped beside Kenise who cocked one leg and leaned forward, resting her forearm on the car roof.

Kenise glanced over at her, smirked that hideous smirk, then waltzed round the back of the car to get in the passenger seat, her ribald laughter slicing a path of hate through Faith's psyche—laughter that said Faith's plan to snatch the customer had failed.

That bitch would pay.

Faith hoped Kenise got a dose of the clap and was out of commission for days. Then again, no, because Reggie might go with her again, bring it home, and spread it to Faith.

Instead, she imagined the punter slitting Kenise's throat and leaving her to die on the side of a lonely road. Faith smiled as the car drove away, hoping to God her wish came true.

Chapter Twenty-Five

At twenty to ten, Laura Gardiner left her sewing club, waving like a maniac at her friends as they each walked to their respective cars. She loved going to the community centre, her one night a week away from home and the drudge she'd become. Here, for three hours, she got to be her old self, someone without burdens, no one banging on at her to do this or that. She learned new skills every time, and the laughter raised her spirits.

She got in her car, a cloud hanging over her now she had to go home. She wasn't treated badly as such, just taken for granted, and she'd lost herself somewhat over the years. Lost her ability to stand up for herself and say no.

She ran her own business—not that she paid any taxes, mind—repurposing old clothes, giving them a revamp and selling them on Vinted. She made a tidy sum to be fair, which supplemented her benefits. With four kids to feed and a husband who could eat a scabby dog on the daily, she had to provide for them somehow. Families were expensive. John couldn't work, his gammy ankle saw to that, an injury he'd sustained at his old job, resulting in his foot being turned inwards. He waited for an operation, but with the NHS how it was these days, she doubted it'd be anytime soon. Laura claimed Universal Credit, and John got PIP, and with her extra Vinted income she could at least make ends meet.

She took her phone out of her bag and checked her messages. John usually sent her a couple when she was at sewing club, as if to remind her he existed, or maybe, as she'd once cruelly thought, he didn't want her doing anything that didn't involve him, didn't want her having something just for herself, so he had to butt in.

She had a text from him — of course she bloody did — and one from Faith. Maybe she had some more clothes to pass on. The last lot had still had tags on, so Laura hadn't had to amend them, tart them up. She opened Faith's message and frowned. Her heart seemed to drop then bounce back up, and her skin switched from the warmth of anger regarding John to the cold of fear.

"What the fuck?"

She read it again. Who was Bungle? And what the hell was Faith doing getting involved with Mrs Whitehall when she lived on Cardigan?

She threw the phone on the passenger seat and gunned the engine, peeling out of the car park. An alarm binged, so she put her seat belt on one-handed, navigating the quiet street, panicking her arse off. Should she go to Sneddon's garden and get Faith? Or do what she'd been asked?

Rumour had it you had to go and see Lisa or Debbie at The Angel if you didn't have the twins' number and needed to get hold of them, so she drove there, parking opposite. Taking her phone, she legged it across the street and into the pub, scanning the bar staff. Lisa, who always seemed to be there—when did she ever have time off?—laughed at the end of the bar with Sonny Bates, and Laura bolted down there, shoving through rowdy customers and treading on someone's toe.

"I need to speak to you. It's urgent." Out of breath and frightened, Laura clutched the bar for support.

"Hold up, love," Sonny said. "What's got you all in a lather?"

She ignored him and brought her phone to life, showing Lisa Faith's message.

"Shit. Hang on." Lisa walked off through a door behind the bar.

Laura shifted from foot to foot, her anxiety spiking.

"Let me see that." Sonny drew her phone towards him by grabbing her wrist. He read the message. "Oh dear. She's fucked."

"What do you mean?" Laura's heartbeat ramped up.

"One, this message was sent ages ago, so if she's still in this Sneddon's garden, I'll eat my hat, and two, Faith was given a Cheshire, and you know what that means. Who did it. They're not going to help her."

"Will you come round Sneddon's with me, then? Please, I can't leave her there."

"What, and help a woman the twins won't want to help, get involved in Whitehall business? Sorry, but I like my job and my wages. Faith's on her own, and don't you go plonking your size fives in it either. Whatever she's got herself into, it's her fault. Go home. You've passed the message on, so let The Brothers decide what to do with the information."

Laura swallowed. This was bloody horrible, walking away. No, she wasn't fond of Faith, but the woman had just lost her son, so surely George and Greg would go round, wouldn't they?

Lisa came back. "I've sent a message. No reply, so they're likely busy, and there's no guarantee they'll have Faith's back anyway, not after what *she* did."

Laura didn't know what she was on about, but it sounded as if Faith had pissed the twins off. Not wanting to do the same by poking into something they'd possibly want left alone, she thanked Lisa and left.

On her way home, her mind threw out possible scenarios. This Bungle could be hiding in the street, so Laura was better off going indoors and forgetting all about this. Sneddon might have found Faith in his garden and taken her inside so she was safe. The twins might not have answered Lisa yet because they'd already found out about Faith's problem somehow.

Laura parked in front of her house and, to appease her conscience, messaged Faith back.

LAURA: I'VE TOLD LISA.

Her phone remained silent.

Laura went inside, guilt roaring through her, but she had kids to protect, and messing with The Brothers would bring trouble to her door. She stretched a smile out so John didn't twig anything was up and entered the living room.

He frowned at her. "Did you forget to go to the chippy?"

"Shit, I didn't see your message. I'll go now."

"Don't worry, I'll stick some oven chips in."

Why didn't you just do that before instead of making more work for me? "No, no, I'll go. I missed dinner, didn't I, so I need something."

She walked out, shitting herself in case this Bungle bloke appeared. The street was empty, so she got in her Mini and drove slowly past Faith's. In a gap between parked cars, she spotted something. Curious, telling herself to drive on and not get out, she ignored her voice of reason and left the car. Went over.

A handbag on the pavement.

Faith's.

"Oh God…"

It must be bad for Faith to have left her bag. The bloody thing was usually glued to her hip whenever she was out and about. Laura picked it up and took it to her car. She drove on, making it to the chippy just before half ten when it shut. Good, it meant she'd get loads of extra chips because they wouldn't want to throw them away. She checked John's message in case he wanted a sausage—he did, what a surprise, the gannet— then placed her order, getting a few cod bites for herself. Nothing for the kids, they'd be in bed.

Back in the car with the food packages, she felt bad but poked around in Faith's handbag, the illuminated sign from the chippy giving her ample light. As well as the usual, a phone. A passport and birth certificate in a transparent plastic folder. An envelope. Curious, she opened it and just about choked. Money. Lots of it. She counted one of the stacks and felt sick. A grand, and there were five all told.

She slid the envelope into the brown chip bag and pondered her deceit all the way home. That money could have been stolen by anyone before she'd found it, the handbag being out on the street like that. No one would know it was her.

Struggling with her need to be good and put the envelope back in the handbag, she thought of the school trips she had to pay for, her eldest wanting to go to Wales, another child slated to visit the Eden Project, then came the idea of topping the leccy meter up to see them through the winter, new coats and boots, all sorts. If Mrs Whitehall had got hold of Faith, it didn't look good, did it, and Faith certainly wouldn't need the money if she'd been caught for whatever the fuck she'd done.

Laura entered her street and slowed near where she'd found the bag. She cast her gaze around to check for any neighbours watching. Pressed the button to lower the windows and leaned over as far as she could to toss the handbag out. It landed in the road by the kerb, but it would have to do, she wasn't taking the risk of getting out to put it on the pavement. She continued on to her house, parked, and stashed the envelope in her coat pocket. She'd hide it later.

John didn't need to know about it. She could make out she'd saved for the school trips out of her Vinted stash if he wanted to know how she'd paid for them outright in the morning, and besides, if she shared her theft with him, he'd only want to take the cash down the bookies, saying he could double his money. He was a sod for that, and she was sick of him using her Vinted earnings to fund his bad habit, which included smoking proper cigarettes, which cost a fortune these days, instead of the cheaper baccy.

When she thought about it, he was a selfish prick really.

For once in her life, Laura was going to keep a secret from him. About Faith's message, which she now deleted, and about the money.

It was better that way.

Chapter Twenty-Six

Austin had been treated to a slap-up meal earlier in the Noodle and Tiger—steak, chips, peppercorn sauce, a grilled tomato, peas, jam roly-poly and custard for pudding. The twins had talked to him like he was their mate now. He wasn't sure whether to trust them yet, but he'd relaxed somewhat, listening to their stories, antics when they'd been younger, up-and-coming gangsters with a need to prove they were faces, adept enough to convince the other leaders they could take over Cardigan, even though they hadn't been the next in line to run it. He'd pondered whether they were telling him of their exploits so he further understood how fucking mental in the head they were, what they could do to him if he crossed them, but they hadn't needed to do that. He'd heard the rumours, thanks, he knew *exactly* what they were like, and he'd cringed at the fact he'd been rude to them that time they'd come round his place about Goldie. He'd been so fucked up on drink and the mess he'd made of his life that he'd allowed himself to be a wanker.

Now, he was on his way to The Whitehall Estate, a lump of sick in his throat that wouldn't go down no matter how much he tried to swallow it, a glut of anxiety in his stomach that twisted and churned. The twins followed in a taxi of all things—were they taking the piss? He didn't have a posh black cab like them, just his car, and he wondered if they'd lend the cab to him until he could afford his own.

No, *he'd* be taking the piss if he asked them that. Best not to get too cosy or expect too much.

They'd let him off with his life, and he ought to be grateful for that.

Nerves spread, seeming to nip at his muscles and flounce through his blood until he proper wanted to throw up. He'd foregone seeing the kids today, sending a message to Maxine, apologising for being a no-show, and she'd replied that she'd been waiting for the day he lost interest and let them down, surprised he hadn't done it long before now. He'd told her that wasn't the case, he had a new job and was out for a meal with his bosses, that he'd be giving her more child support, but she'd flipped him the bird in an emoji and told him to go and fuck himself with a sharp stick.

When he got paid for his taxi job, he'd buy her some flowers and the kids a toy each to make up for it. And tomorrow, he'd definitely be at her house, four o'clock on the dot, like usual. Of course, she could refuse to let him see the children, and he wouldn't blame her, but he prayed she'd have calmed down by then.

He crossed the borders from Cardigan to Moon to Whitehall, and his stomach cramped. The last thing he needed was a shit now, but he really thought he was going to crap himself. He kept driving, taking his mind off his fear by looking in the rearview. The headlights behind flashed, and he wasn't sure what to do. Keep driving or pull over?

Austin flicked his hazards on and parked outside a small row of shops.

His phone bleeped.

GG: WHAT HAVE YOU STOPPED FOR?

AUSTIN: I THOUGHT YOU WANTED ME TO. YOU FLASHED.

GG: JESUS, I WAS JUST LETTING YOU KNOW WE WERE STILL BEHIND YOU. GET A FUCKING MOVE ON, YOU PLONKER, SHE WON'T LIKE YOU BEING LATE.

Feeling stupid, Austin drove off. How was he supposed to know what the bloody signal meant? Frustrated with himself for being a dick, plus annoyed at George, he followed the satnav's instructions. It guided him to the outskirts of the estate, down a tree-lined avenue, woods either side, no houses around. Except at the end. Small pockets of square light beckoned him forward, and going by the amount of windows, she lived in a fucking big gaff.

At the junction, he glanced left and right. Several large homes stood in a row, all fancy behind high iron fences and gates.

"Turn right," the satnav lady said.

He obeyed, wanting to go home. He had a shedload of drugs in the boot and was dropping it off to a woman who was rumoured to be a nutter when the fancy took her. Hopefully someone at the gate would take it off his hands and he could sod off sharpish.

"In one hundred yards, your destination is on the right."

He checked left, nothing but woodland. He crawled along, squinting to make out a house number on plaques attached to the gates, but it seemed these residents didn't want to give the postman a hand in knowing where to deliver their letters. Each gate had a metal postbox, so maybe the numbers were on those.

"You have reached your destination."

Austin stopped and stared through the fence bars. The house, had to be about ten bedrooms, resembled a stately home. A couple of German shepherds and a rottweiler came to the gate and poked their noses through the gaps, teeth bared.

"Fuck me sideways…"

Heart rate chuntering along, he eased the car closer to the gate. Glanced in the rearview. The taxi had parked in front of the house next door, headlights off. Austin got out, legs going weird on him, and approached an intercom on the gatepost. A camera above it whirred to life and moved, pointing down at him, a cyclops eye staring, giving him the willies. One of the dogs growled, setting the others off, and he reached out gingerly to press the button.

"Austin Hunt with a parcel for Mrs Whitehall," he said and let the button go.

"Come through when the gates open."

Shit, they wanted him on the property? He got back in the car, wishing he could abandon this and fuck right off, but the twins were watching, and he couldn't let them down. A bad feeling exploded inside him, and as he drove through the open gateway, he couldn't work out if it was the fear of taking drugs to a woman he'd forced Faith to steal from or the natural unease of doing something illegal.

He stopped the car, unsure if he was supposed to go closer to the house. The lack of instructions was doing his head in, and absurdly, he wanted to cry. He stared at the rearview, and the gates closing behind him sent his lungs into spasm. He couldn't catch a breath, and panic took hold. It further ramped up at the sight of a figure emerging out of the darkness, becoming a silhouette in the beam of his headlights: legs, a torso, and a neck visible, but no face. A gloved hand beckoned him forward, and the person walked on ahead. A bloke, going by the shape — someone as large as a wrestler, or at least it appeared that way.

Austin, paranoid his foot would slip on the pedal and he'd jerk the car forward, running the wrestler down, concentrated on moving forward. The driveway wasn't that long, but it seemed to take ages to go up it. The man stopped and gestured for Austin to get out.

He thought about the hounds that hadn't exactly given him a nice greeting. He'd bet they'd be snapping their jaws by now, wanting to take a chunk out of his arse. Lowering the window, he called, "The dogs…"

"They won't hurt you unless I tell them to."

Fucking hell, they're trained to attack?

Austin left the car, wanting to look back to see if the twins were still there but not daring to give them away. They'd said they didn't need Whitehall to know they'd followed him. Something about not wanting to show her they didn't trust her anymore. That hadn't made

Austin feel any better when George had said it, but they'd promised to have his back.

"Give me your keys," Wrestler said.

Austin swallowed and took them from his pocket, holding them out.

Wrestler snatched them. "Mrs Whitehall would like to meet you. Go through the front door and turn left."

"The package…"

"I'll deal with that."

Austin—his legs didn't belong to him anymore, they'd turned into spaghetti—all but staggered up to the house. He was going to fuck this up, he knew it. Blurt something out that he shouldn't because he was nervous. She'd take it the wrong way, maybe get one of her men to smack him about a bit to teach him a lesson. He'd have to drive home with a swollen black eye.

He pushed the door open. A massive foyer, the floor tiles so shiny two sideboards were mirrored in them. A staircase ahead and centred, with fancy swirls as handrails, gold, patterns carved into them. Royal-purple carpet. A landing ran across the top, antique furniture on display. He counted the doors to his right—seven—then did the same on the left—five. The one to his immediate left was a double, only one of them open. Through the slice of space, he took in a white fireplace, flames leaping in the grate, and a cream fabric sofa, scrolls for arms. A red carpet, a huge fluffy white rug in the centre, and a fucking dobie sat on it, ears pinned up, its beady eyes assessing him.

"Shanghai won't bite," a woman said.

Jesus Christ. Could she see him in a reflection, or did the house have cameras and she watched him on her phone? He moved towards the door, sure his fear would reach the dog and send it wild, and entered the room.

She sat on another sofa, her clothes cream, so it appeared she was just a head, hands, and feet in big bastard Doc Marten boots. He blinked to readjust his sight, and her outline became clearer.

"Mr Hunt," she said, one side of her face painted orange from the light of the flames. "I take it you've brought the goods." She laughed. "Of *course* you have. You'd be a fool not to."

He smiled for want of something better to do, his lips wobbly, and wasn't sure what was the best thing going forward. Stay where he was? Sit?

"You can have the other sofa."

He walked over there, skirting the dobie, and perched on the edge.

She glared at him. "Why did you think it was okay to steal from me?"

Oh fuck. *Fuck.* "I...I've told the twins. They...they get I was forced into it. I was desperate. Benny Bender, he—"

"Don't you have a mind of your own? Are you saying Benny strong-armed you into taking my money?"

With Benny dead, the lender couldn't refute what Austin said, so he *could* go down that road and blame him, but George had told him to stick as close to the truth as possible. "I do, and unfortunately, I chose the wrong route. I wanted Benny to fuck—to go away, get off my back, and this woman called Satin, I used to know her from school, and she said there was money in the safe in the brothel and it'd be easy to nick it."

"So you're saying my employee, my right-hand girl, told you to steal from me. Can you not take any accountability for yourself? Do you always blame others for your actions?"

"No, I mean yes, but I'm trying not to anymore. I'm getting therapy and everything. She *did* tell me about it, though. Otherwise, how else would I have known to get hold of Faith? I didn't know where she worked until Satin told me."

"Faith is dead. Would you like to see?"

Oh shit, was she here? Did this nutter have her body somewhere? "Um, not really."

"Let me show you."

A large flat-screen TV sprang to life above the fireplace—who the hell had turned it on? Faith, or what was left of her, appeared. Her torso in a pool of blood on lino, so maybe a kitchen or bathroom, her head chopped off, the face turned to the left. Her severed arms and legs lay in a tangle beside her, blood-smeared and so sodding awful he battled being sick. Blood matted her hair, which gleamed from the wetness beneath what he supposed were overhead lights, and the stump of her neck...

Austin heaved and slapped a hand over his mouth, swallowing vomit.

"Not a pretty sight, is she? That's what happens when you cross me. You don't get a very nice ending. You've got The Brothers to thank for you still being allowed to breathe at the minute, although I do feel it's rather rude that they still sent you as their deliveryman, everything considered. Rubbing salt in the wound somewhat, but they did assure me they'd chosen you before they became aware of what you'd done, so there's that."

"I'm sorry," he choked out. "So fucking sorry."

"People usually are when they're shown what can happen. When they face the consequences of their actions. It stings a little, doesn't it?"

She was definitely off her nut, the way she spoke so calmly, as if Faith's remains weren't on that telly, weren't shouting at Austin for him to look at them again.

"You can go now," she said. "But I'll see you very soon."

He couldn't get out of there fast enough, her titter of a laugh chasing him into the foyer. He ran so fast he skidded and yanked the front door open, stopping short at the sight of those bloody German shepherds leering at him, hackles raised, teeth on show.

"Oh God…"

"Belgium and Japan, come!" Mrs Whitehall called.

Clearly, she named her dogs after places—had she visited them, or did she plan to?—and what an inane thought to go through is head when he faced jaws that could rip his bollocks off inside a second if she gave the order. Meek now — *creepy bastards* — the dogs padded past him. And how the fuck did she know which dogs they were, because the rottweiler wasn't in sight. Where was it, waiting in the darkness with Wrestler? She must have cameras everywhere.

Austin pelted outside, desperate to find his car. He glanced over at the road — the twins were still there, thank fuck — then darted to the right, legging it to the end of the house in case Wrestler had taken it round there. He rushed into the blackness, blindly heading into fuck knew what, coming out at the rear, entering a beautiful garden lit up with Victorian lampposts, weird hedges in the shape of those sodding dogs. Maybe there was a garage on the other side, and Wrestler had hidden the car inside so no neighbours saw him taking the goods out of the boot.

Austin sprinted along the patio, slowing at spotting the rottweiler. He stopped dead, his heart hurting, a pain shooting through it. "Jesus fucking wept, no."

Mrs Whitehall appeared at patio doors to his right, and he jumped. He looked at her. She smiled at him, head cocked, and it really shit him up. She had more than a screw loose, her basket short of not just a sandwich but the whole fucking picnic.

What should he do? Hope the dog didn't lunge for him? Back away? Go round the front and get the twins' attention? The gate was likely locked, so he'd have to climb over, but with the rottweiler on his tail, it'd give him the impetus to scale it.

Mrs Whitehall stared behind Austin and nodded.

The smack to the back of his head knocked him out cold.

Chapter Twenty-Seven

*R*eggie's behaviour had got worse. He treated Faith like a skivvy and barked orders more often than usual, although at times, he smiled to himself, his face morphing from an angry grimace to a softer expression, one she recognised from when she'd first met him and he'd looked at her as if he loved her. Who did he think about during those times? Was it Kenise?

Unfortunately, the bitch hadn't caught the clap and she'd been out in the lane every night since their confrontation. Faith hadn't brought it up with Reggie because one, he'd deny it, or two, he'd rub it in her face that he had *been shagging that woman. She couldn't face either response, yet she wanted to know if it was an on-going thing. She'd be able to gauge how close he was to leaving her, if he even was—and God, she hoped he was.*

Would he take Lemon, though? She couldn't bear that. Maybe that was why she'd kept quiet. She didn't want to run the risk of losing her son. He was the only person who'd ever acted as if he truly, truly couldn't be without her. His dependency on her fed her soul, gladdened her days, and she wanted more of it. To have felt so…unimportant as a child, to then having her own child treating her as if she was the most amazing thing on the planet—she could get addicted to that. The more she indulged him, the more he clung to her.

She shivered in the lane, the winter a cold one. Her skimpy clothing under her long, beige fake fur coat, one Reggie had found in a charity shop and flung at her, was on display because she hadn't done the buttons up. In her experience, punters wanted to see the goods, although Reggie had suggested that men liked to imagine, to unwrap the parcel before they sampled what was beneath.

Diamond got out of a red car and seemed to float over, likely high on something or other. That particular customer was free with the drugs, so she'd probably taken some instead of being paid. Diamond's life outside the lane, chaotic and something Faith doubted she'd be able to cope with, meant the woman wanted nothing more than to block it all out.

"That man's well decent," she said, her pupils blown.

"Did you get any money?" Faith asked.

"Nah, just a bit of coke."

"But you need to eat, pay the rent."

"Food's for wimps, and as for the rent, I got kicked out today, so I'm kipping round her squat." She flapped a hand in Jazzy's direction. "There's four in our bedroom so it's warmer at night, all that breathing and stuff."

The thought of that churned Faith's stomach. If she were a nicer person, she'd offer Diamond their spare room, but in truth, she didn't want her druggy arse near Lemon, and Reggie would put a block on it anyway.

A car crept along. Faith tensed, as she always did now, if the headlights were square, the car white.

301

Thankfully, a black hatchback drew up to the kerb, and the driver lowered his window and smiled at her.

"How much, love?"

"Christmas special," she said. "Fifty quid."

"Get in."

Glad to get out of the cold, she sat in his car and put her seat belt on. He smiled at her, raised the window, and drove away.

"I need to park somewhere so I'm not seen," he said. "Married, see. I'm new round here, so can you direct me where to go?"

"The trading estate will be empty. Take a left here."

He followed her directions. "How long have you been doing your job?"

She was used to this type of conversation, no longer surprised that these men didn't want to talk pervy like she'd first assumed. A lot of them wanted to be heard without getting nagging responses, and she knew how they felt. Reggie nagged. "Long enough."

"Like that, is it? What did you do before?"

"Go right here." She pointed. "I worked in a factory."

"Better pay doing this, isn't it?"

"Yes, but it isn't something I'd choose to do."

"I feel for you, I really do, but if people like you didn't exist, I'd be shit out of luck. Where to next?"

"Right again, then we're there. If you go behind the tyre place, no one will see us."

He seemed nice. Calm and friendly, none of that leering business that gave her the creeps. He had smooth hands, hands men in offices had, and his nails had been clipped. He smelled all right, too, an expensive aftershave if she was any judge, although his car and clothes didn't give the impression he was loaded. His well-groomed moustache must have recently been trimmed, because the hairs were blunt-ended and in a complete straight line. She always took a good look at punters, although in the rapist's case, she hadn't done anything about it. His face was burned in her mind, glaring at her as soon as she shut her eyes to go to sleep.

The customer rounded the back of Todd's Tyres, reversed close to the building, and parked. His headlights splashed onto the view ahead, a line of frosted trees that separated the trading estate from a farmer's field which stretched towards a dual carriageway. The glow of red taillights gave her a measure of comfort. This was why she'd told him to come here. If she had to run, she knew where she was going. Half a mile along on the carriageway stood a petrol garage, more comfort.

He switched the internal light on and looked at her, turning the engine off, the headlights dousing.

"Do you like being told what to do?" he asked.

"You're the customer," she said.

"What does the fifty pounds get me?"

"Penetrative sex, condom, no touching my breasts, no kissing, no intimacy." If anyone had told her she'd say that without cringing, she'd never have believed them. She'd have said she wouldn't say it full stop, yet here she was.

"Can I hurt you?"

She stared at him, her heart clattering. "W-what?"

"Can I hurt you? I always think it's polite to ask before I do that."

She scrabbled for the door handle, knowing full well it was pointless; she hadn't got away from the rapist, so she wouldn't get away from him. Her skin, going cold despite the car being warm from the heater being on, then broke out in a clammy sweat. He stroked the back of her hair softly, and it freaked her out. She raised a hand to flick him away from her, instinct taking over.

"I don't want sex with you," he said. "I was being nice by talking about your job, asking questions, making conversation. I just want to hurt you, that's all."

She gritted her teeth. "Take your hand off my head."

"I want to lick your hair. Will you let me do that?"

She jerked her elbow out and hit him in the chest. It didn't faze him.

"Please? One little lick?"

Every part of her, revolted by his request, seemed to shrivel and die, leaving her arms and legs numb, unresponsive, yet her brain was alive, synapses firing, scenario after scenario blasting through her mind.

"That was quick," he said.

She frowned, shaking her head to get some sense into it instead of images of rape and mutilation. "What are you on about?"

"How fast you accepted the inevitable. So many women fight me, and I don't understand why."

"Because you're fucking scary!"

"I don't mean to be."

If it wasn't for Lemon, she'd give up. She'd let this man kill her, take her away from this nasty life, but she had to get out of this car, for him.

She thought about what he'd just said. He'd sounded confused about why she'd be scared. Was he just misunderstood? "What do you mean by wanting to hurt me?"

"I want to put my arm across your throat so you can't breathe."

She dared to look into his eyes. She needed to know if he was crazy. But he appeared normal, just a nice, kind bloke. Was that worse? That he was someone nobody would suspect of being like this?

"What else?" she asked.

"That's it."

"What about the sex?"

"I already said, not with you. I'll sort myself out."

What was this, some kind of sex game where he choked her while he pulled on his dick?

"Will I be alive after?"

"Yes."

"So is this…is this that weird erotic shit people are talking about?"

"Yes."

"Then you need to work on your approach, articulate what you want better." She slumped in relief. "You really frightened me! I thought you wanted to kill me."

"I'm sorry."

He leaned across and sniffed her hair, then licked it. This was the weirdest thing a punter had ever done to her, and it brought on a rush of nausea. He let her hair go and undid his trousers, freeing his erection. He straightened his other arm and pushed it against her throat, and she closed her eyes. Willed it to be over soon. *The pressure reminded her of Reggie choking her against the larder door that time, and panic rose, threading through her chest. His jerking jostled her, and she held back a heave, breathing through her nostrils as taking air through her mouth felt like too much of a struggle. Tears fell, hot down her cheeks, and they dripped over her chin and down her neck, likely soaking into his coat sleeve.*

I'm doing this for Lemon. So we can get away.

"*That's it, cry,*" he said. "*Cry.*"

He pushed harder. She couldn't breathe now and lifted her hands to wrench his arm off her, but it wouldn't budge. Her face heated, the panic growing, and weird spots of light danced in her vision.

"*I won't kill you, I promise.*"

Blackness crowded in, and she succumbed to it.

She woke, cold and shivering, something wet against her bare legs. Grass? A chilly breeze soughed over her face, and she sat up, peering into the darkness. Her throat, so sore, meant it was hard to swallow, and prickly pain lanced it. She pushed up off the ground, disorientated for a moment, trying to work out where

she was. She stood behind Todd's Tyres, only the trees for company.

Had he driven off because he thought he'd killed her?

She patted for her bag — there it was, still hanging across her body — and she staggered around the front of the building so she could check its contents by the light of a lamppost. She dug around inside, thankful everything was still in there, as well as five hundred quid in loose notes.

She stared, uncomprehending. He'd paid her that much?

Why leave her here, though? Was it more than a sex game? Had he played out what it would be like to kill someone, to dump a body, ready for when he had the guts to actually do it?

Why did bad things keep happening to her?

She ran, her ankle turning twice, but she kept going. Lungs burning, her throat aching, she reached the lane and rushed to a nearby bench. She sat to catch her breath, to make sense of what the fuck had just happened, but she had nothing.

What she did know was, she couldn't do this anymore. The risks were too great.

A pipe dream, though, giving it all up, because Reggie wouldn't let her.

And besides, she'd got used to earning a lot of money. Going back to a factory wage was out of the question. For someone who'd vowed never to let a man touch her after Tim, she was doing a bloody good job of encouraging them to do just that.

Chapter Twenty-Eight

George had been watching through night-vision binoculars, the taxi stuffy, his irritation levels spiking. The big bloke in a balaclava moving Austin's car into one of the garages, plus Austin having to go inside the house, had waved two red flags. All right, he could get on board with the car thing; neighbours might come by and spot what was going on, and there was no sense in having the police coming round and asking questions. Balaclava might have clocked their taxi, so again, he was making sure nothing was seen. But Mrs Whitehall didn't need to speak to Austin. George could understand why he'd gone indoors. Balaclava had probably said something menacing, giving him no choice. He could have hinted he had a gun, so Austin wouldn't have risked running to the taxi and getting shot. Whitehall was likely giving him a warning in her usual acerbic way, something George had once loved, but now, since she'd gone against their agreement, he didn't like it.

"We were stupid to send Austin," he said. "Hold on, there's movement."

George concentrated. A dark Transit backed out of another garage, whoever drove doing a three-point turn and pointing the bonnet towards the gates. George zoomed in on the driver. Balaclava, who took the mask off.

"Jesus wept, that's Lincoln's man."

"What?"

"The driver."

"Are you fucking serious? Is he moonlighting or something? Playing two sides?"

"I don't know. Get hold of Lincoln and ask. He's going to go mental."

Lincoln, another leader, wasn't someone to cross. When he heard about his employee being here, he'd lose his shit.

The lights went out in the house, and Mrs Whitehall emerged, a German shepherd either side of her, a pinscher going on ahead, as if it were a scout, protecting her.

"I don't like the look of this. What's with the dogs?" He paused, thinking this through. "Austin might not even be in the Transit." George told Greg what he'd seen since his brother had been texting. "Get hold of Moon and Tick-Tock. We'll follow the van, and you can tell them where we're going. We need witnesses if Whitehall's being dodgy."

Whitehall got in the front of the van, the dogs jumping in with her. It'd be a bit of a squeeze along with the driver, even though it was the kind with three seats. A shepherd plonked itself on her lap, obscuring George's view of her face. The van cruised down the driveway, the gates opening automatically. George lobbed the binoculars at Greg.

"Ouch, that hit my lip. If it swells up..."

"Christ, get over it." George prepared to tail them.

The van went left, heading straight towards the taxi. George and Greg lowered in their seats and dipped their heads. The shepherd still blocked Whitehall's face, so she couldn't see them yet, but if she turned her head when they went past…

Fuck, fuck, fuck…

"They've gone," Greg said.

George stared into the rearview. Austin's mug appeared in one of the van's rear windows, and he made a slitting motion across his throat.

"Did you see that?" George asked.

"Yep. I'm going to fucking kill her."

George waited for the van to veer into the tree-lined avenue. Having to turn around wasted time, but he got on with it. He checked the mirror. "The gates are closing. Must be on a sensor." He gunned down the street and careened around the corner.

"Slow down!" Greg bollocked him. "You'll get us noticed. She knows we have a taxi. Another bloody stupid mistake, bringing it."

"I forgot, all right? And it wasn't like you said anything at the time."

"We should have picked our van, put new decals on the sides."

"Yet you didn't mention it. Now we look like a pair of bumbling idiots."

"Whatever."

George followed for a few miles, annoyed with himself. They entered The Whitehall Estate proper, going through a residential area and coming out on a main road. A mile or so along, the van went right onto a trading estate, and George had a horrible feeling about where they were going.

"Her fucking abattoir. Tell Moon and Tick-Tock."

"They might not get here in time. Their estates are miles away."

"Then we'll have to deal with it ourselves, won't we. Has Lincoln replied yet?"

"No, and I'd have said if he had."

"Wonder why he's ignoring you? Maybe he's that naffed off he's got in his motor and is on his way to Whitehall's. Tell him we're at her abattoir. He can catch his bloke in the act."

The van took a left onto the access track to the abattoir, and George continued on the road they were on, parking down the side of Good Night

Mattresses. They got out, George taking machine guns and ammunition from the boot—he wasn't fucking about here.

"I want her men dead but Whitehall alive," he whispered. "She needs to be held accountable in front of the other leaders."

They crept into the night, down the access road, George inviting Mad and Ruffian to the party.

Chapter Twenty-Nine

Wrestler hauled Austin out of the van by the scruff of his neck, dragging him towards a roller door which slowly rose. Just like at the house, shit happened without anyone being around to press any buttons, and he assumed Mrs Whitehall had given an order from the front seat via a text. Someone must be inside. How many were waiting to ambush him? What was she going to do to him? Was she going to make out he'd done a runner with the drugs and demand her money back off the twins, then sell the coke anyway?

The back of his head hurt; he'd touched it on the journey, a big fucking lump, slightly wet where whatever he'd been bashed with had split the skin. The hadn't even been tied up, but it wasn't like he could strangle the driver from behind because a wire mesh separated the front from the back. If it hadn't, those ruddy dogs would have bitten his hands off anyway. One of them had pressed his nose to the mesh and snorted snot at him.

The soft panting and a yip of excitement told him the dogs followed. The scent of old meat mixed with cleaning products slapped him in the face the second Wrestler guided him along a delivery bay. Through a door ahead, Wrestler marched him down a corridor, then took a left into a room that belonged in Austin's nightmares. Or should that be a fridge half the size of a netball court?

Pigs and cows hung from hooks, their skin removed, the pigs presenting as pale forms, the cows a combination of fat and meat on show. The cows had no heads, but the pigs… It seemed they stared at him even in death, upside down, their front trotters half a metre from the floor. He glanced up. A pulley system, so he guessed the carcases were lowered when it was time to load them for delivery.

"String him up," Whitehall barked from behind.

Austin jumped from fear, his stupid heart going like the clappers. Wrestler snapped cuffs on, Austin's wrists complaining at them being too tight. A hook came down in the middle of a row of pigs, the clank of the mechanism loud and obnoxious. What was Wrestler going to do, drape the chain between the cuffs over the hook? Austin hoped it would break with his weight. The idea of those cuffs digging in even more than they already were, the gnaw of them on his skin…

Wrestler pushed Austin past some pigs to where the hook descended. He lifted Austin's hood, held the hook inside it, and waited for the wire to go back up. The hook tugged at the hood, and Austin quickly grabbed the neck of his sweatshirt before it had a chance to choke him. His feet left the floor, his hands rising along with the material, then, with a violent snap, the wire went faster, and Austin's bunched hands slammed into his throat. He dangled, hating the nasty sensation of his sweatshirt ruching under his armpits, his knuckles tight against his Adam's apple. He swung and spun for a moment, finally going still, and stared down at Mrs Whitehall who came closer, standing in front of a pig.

She looked up at him. "I was playing a game when The Brothers so rudely interrupted it. The games fuel me, calm me, and I need them, so abandoning this one isn't an option because I've been *extremely* irate of late. I was a good girl and didn't bring Faith here, so I should be congratulated for that."

She waited.

What, was *he* supposed to congratulate her?"

"Err, well done?" he said.

She smiled. "I *could* have stopped, taken you out of it and only toyed with Faith, but I didn't want to give you up. They'll be cross, those twins, but I don't particularly care. They made it obvious they were following us just now, so I suspect they'll barge in any second and try to put a halt to this. They'll have guns, and they'll shoot, but so will my men."

Austin hadn't seen anyone but Wrestler. Men peeled out from behind some cows, weaving between the bodies, nudging some of them with their shoulders so the carcases rocked. All the blokes held guns, some trained on him, some pointing towards the door.

"We should get on with it, really." She sighed, as though the game coming to an end wasn't a happy event. "Let's start with his tackle. Silver, you do it."

Austin, shocked and frightened, battled to relieve the pressure on his throat, his upper arms sticking outwards so he could keep the neckline down a bit. A man, presumably Silver, tucked his gun into his waistband and came over to undo the button and draw the zip down on Austin's jeans. He could see why he was called Silver. The bloke was fucking huge, a silverback gorilla. Silver tugged Austin's jeans and boxers down to his knees, and Austin willed his bladder not to let go.

"This reminds me of Bungle with Faith," Mrs Whitehall said. "The yanking down of her leggings and knickers."

Oh God, were they repeating what had happened to her? What had he done? Was this part of the game, both players receiving the same punishment?

"She was raped, by the way." Mrs Whitehall sounded unaffected by it. "But you won't have to go through that. None of my men like arse." She laughed, the echo of it bouncing off the dead animals. "I just want your dick and balls so I can see what they look like when they come out of the mincer. A test run before your whole body goes in it."

The mincer? What the fuck is she on?

He prayed The Brothers hurried up. Imagining the pain of his dick and bollocks being hacked off brought on a wave of nausea.

Silver produced a knife, lightly scraping the blade up and down Austin's cock. It'd be shrivelled from his fear, and any second now, he expected Whitehall to cackle at the size of it. Demean him. Make him feel less of a man.

"Pull it to make it stretch," she said. "Then you'll have a good enough length to slice off." She paused. Tapped one foot. "Where the hell are those twins? I wanted them to see this."

His dick, elongated and wrenched, hurt from the rough handling.

"Actually, I've changed my mind. Just take the foreskin off for now as a little taster."

The cold bite of the knife cutting his skin had Austin drawing his legs up and screaming. His eyes watered, and he clenched his teeth, momentarily forgetting to pull his neckline down, choking from his knuckle pressure. Wet heat, the burn of agony...would he bleed out? He panicked at that and dared to look down. Silver hadn't lopped it right off, he'd just cut four fifths of the way round. It dangled below his cock, a circle of blood-soaked skin hanging by a thread.

Austin threw up. Silver stepped back just in time, and some of Austin's dinner landed on the floor.

Whitehall squealed in pleasure. "Oh, is it too much? But we've only just started."

Austin blinked, spitting to get the remaining sick out of his mouth. He heaved again, his stomach cramping.

"Let's leave him to contemplate what else is on the way," she said to no one in particular, then to Wrestler, "You can tell him what's on the cards. It'll give the twins time to get their arses in gear. I'm so surprised they haven't come in yet, I really am."

She wandered off through the doorway. The other men melted back between the animals, Wrestler going off to the side and returning with a dustpan and brush. Silver collected a mop and bucket, and they worked in silence, not once looking Austin's way. It seemed cleaning up sick and blood didn't faze them. They must have done it so often that it had become normal.

Austin let the tears fall, fuck whether anyone noticed. He was past caring. Would he see his kids again? Maxine? The pain in his cock throbbed, and anger rose, aimed at the twins. What held them up?

He closed his eyes, once more concentrating on relieving the pressure on his throat—at least it would take his focus off his raging dick. Was this the way he'd go out? Were George and Greg in on this? Had Whitehall lied when she'd said she wanted them to see the torture? Was she out there now, wetting herself with them?

He let out a sob.

Wrestler, holding the filth-laden dustpan, took a step closer. "Look, if it's any consolation, just accept you're going to die. Having hope at this point is a waste of time. She's going to get us to skin you alive once your meat and two veg are gone, and we'll leave you hanging here until she decides when you can die. Then she's going to slit your throat and feed you through the mincer."

"She's sick in the head, the mad bitch," Austin seethed.

"Don't let her hear you say that, for fuck's sake."

Silver dumped the mop in the bucket. He elbowed Wrestler. "And don't let her hear *you* giving him sympathy either. Christ, man, have you got a death wish?"

Wrestler ignored him. "You lot, go off and have a break. The boss will be having a little drink before the next round. And that means you an' all, Silver. I'll keep an eye on him."

The men walked between the cows and pigs, filing through the doorway.

Wrestler turned back to Austin. "Listen to me, and don't breathe a word of what I tell you. I'm a mole, understand? I work for another leader. I've contacted him to say what's going on because she's going against the twins. Help is coming."

"Who?" Austin asked, his breathing harsh.

"Ever been to The Lincoln Estate, a small patch close to the north?"

"No."

"Probably best you don't. Lincoln's the biggest nutter you'll ever meet. He keeps to himself, rarely goes to leader meetings if he can help it. He's had his eye on Whitehall ever since her husband got diagnosed—she went off the rails, see, even worse after he died. He gets her estate if she snuffs it. I started working for her just after her fella got told he had cancer, catch my drift?"

Lincoln sent him there. "Yeah."

"Just hold on. It'll all be over soon."

"Are you…taking the…piss?" Austin rasped. "Hold on? It's all I'm fucking doing so I don't choke to death."

Wrestler glanced to the door. "Shh, someone's coming."

Silver appeared, scrutinising them. "What's going on?"

"Fuck all, mate, fuck all." Wrestler took the dustpan and brush out of sight.

Austin digested what he'd been told. That must be why the twins hadn't come in yet. They were having a conflab with this Lincoln bloke, working out the best way to handle this.

Please get in here soon. Please…

Chapter Thirty

*F*aith had called it a night at eleven. She'd earned her quota and then some. The extra, she'd put into the zipped section of her handbag to add to her secret stash when she went to bed. She'd been doing that a lot lately, only giving Reggie the amount he expected, making out she only stayed to service enough men to reach his target. She was going to leave him, run away with Little Lemon and make a new home somewhere *away from London. All the East End did was remind her of Dad, Mum, and Tim, three people who should have wanted the best for her but had treated her appallingly. She knew that now. The love she felt for her son was so all-encompassing that it showed her how she should have been loved by her parents. She had sex with strangers, for God's sake, to help put food in his belly—how many mothers could say they'd done that? Plus she did whatever Reggie said so it limited the amount of times her husband hit her, Lemon a crying witness. She lived a horrible life, one she couldn't stand, and leaving was her only choice.*

Reggie had said he'd kill her, but if he couldn't find her, how could he do it? It was a threat, nothing more, so empty it was laughable. Why had she been so gullible as to believe he'd carry it out? Fear, that's why. She'd taken his words as gospel because if she hadn't, a thump would have punctuated the end of his sentence. She'd had time to think, though, in between customers, to lay it all out logically in her head, to really see her situation. To see Reggie.

He used her to make money. He'd had sex with Kenise. He no longer cared about Faith, perhaps never had. She'd told him about Tim raping her the night they'd first met, and Reggie had grabbed hold of that and run with it. He'd drawn her in, gained her trust, then shit all over it. He'd planned it all, she could see that now.

Clarity was sometimes a bad thing, shining a spotlight on all the wrongs, illuminating all your sins and reminding you of every single path you shouldn't have taken, usually at night when the world rested and all was silent. Other times, though, it was exactly what you needed, a kick up the arse to get your ducks in a row and do something instead of taking whatever was dished out.

She was going to go home and, for one last night, lie beside her husband and pretend she was still the Faith he'd turned her into—a frightened squirrel with him, a nasty piece of work with others. Kenise had been the last straw, and it was time to move on.

She got on the bus and allowed herself to think about everything—her childhood, her teenage years, her foray into marriage, the sex-worker job, Mum, Dad, Clinton, Tarone, Reggie. It had all shaped her, as had the people, and not for the better. She'd become so many versions of herself throughout the years that she hardly recognised who she was these days, or even remembered who she'd been before Dad had killed himself.

Who would she have been if she'd had different parents?

The journey seemed to zip by, or maybe she'd been so inside her head she hadn't noticed the streets whipping past. She got off and walked down her road, her stomach bunching at the thought of having to speak to Reggie. She wasn't in the mood tonight, especially as she'd be arriving before midnight. He'd likely have a go at her for being early. Maybe he'd got drunk on that bottle of rum he'd asked her to buy before she'd gone to work and now snored on the sofa.

She slid her key in the lock and entered, glad he'd left the heating on. Warmth wrapped around her, and she shut the door. Fur coat and shoes off—Jesus, her toes pinched in her stilettos—she poked her head around the living room door. A handbag on the sofa had her frowning, and for one stupid, hopeful moment, she thought Reggie had bought her a new one, but the zip was open, some of the contents on show. A purse, a tampon.

Shit, was Jackie here? Had Reggie finally committed that sin and invited the neighbour here for drinks? Was that why he'd wanted the rum?

A woman's laughter came from upstairs, and she turned from the living room to take stock of the hallway. High-heeled shoes, black. A leather jacket, brown. She couldn't recall seeing Jackie in either of those.

What should she do? If she didn't have Lemon to worry about, she'd walk out and never come back. But she did, and there was no way she'd leave him here.

Quietly, she went upstairs, pausing on the landing at another round of laughter, this time Reggie's.

"You're so fucking sexy," he said.

"Oh, I know, darling."

Faith knew that voice, and it wasn't Jackie's. It made sense now, why Kenise hadn't been at the lane tonight. Because she was here.

Faith opened the bedroom door and stood on the threshold, superciliousness barrelling through her — she wasn't the one in the wrong this time, like he always made her feel, he *was. Not that he'd admit it. He'd say it was his right to fuck whoever the hell he liked.*

The pair of them hadn't even noticed her, too wrapped up in each other. Kenise, naked, sat on top of him, her skin perfect, no sign of cellulite anywhere, her limbs toned, her backside peachy. Everything Faith wasn't. And it hurt.

Kenise rode him, and Reggie finally saw his wife. He smiled at her, and it took a moment for that to register — he thought this was funny? He looked smug, as if he'd wanted *her to catch them.*

Faith turned and went to check on Lemon. Her boy slept soundly, and the thought of picking him up and running entered her mind. But where would she go? Not Mum's, Tim lived there, and her secret stash was in the bedroom with Reggie and that nasty bitch. No, she'd wait until tomorrow, when Reggie was at work. She'd pack the fuck up and run away.

"I told you not to come home early," Reggie called. "Go back out to work, I fancy some new shoes."

"Okay," Faith said. She needed him to think she was still under his thumb, and while she hated what she'd seen, hated that Kenise had come here and defiled her bed, she didn't let the hurt fester. A sense of calm came over her—after all, she knew something Reggie didn't: she was leaving him, an act he'd never think she'd do.

She returned downstairs, her vision blurred, and slipped her feet into her shoes. Her toes pinched more than ever, and she put on her fur coat, something she'd leave behind when she walked out of here for the last time.

Back on the bus, she gathered her mettle, told herself to earn another couple of hundred quid. At the lane, she waited beneath the streetlamp, men in cars slowing then passing her, deeming her not their type without even saying a word. For whatever warped reason, they chose the junkies, but she didn't let it upset her. She was better than them, certainly better than Kenise, and no man would ever make her feel less than again.

A car with tinted windows stopped in front of her, and the window went down an inch. A pair of eyes appeared, shadowed by the interior, so she couldn't make much out.

"Get in," the bloke said.

Did she recognise the accent? East End, deep. No, she'd never been with him before.

She got in the passenger seat and put her safety belt on, then glanced across at him as he pulled away from the kerb.

"Hello, Faith."

Her whole body went cold, and her breath stalled. She stared, trying to take it in, that she was in a car with Tim. Her survival instinct kicked in, and instead of scrabbling to get out of the car, she looked ahead, calculating, going through her future movements in her head. This would end tonight, the fear of him. She'd fix it so he never raped her or anyone else again.

"Lovely to see you," he said. "It's been a long time."

She didn't answer. He didn't seem bothered by that and burbled on about his time in prison, how he'd been beaten up by men who didn't like kiddie fiddlers.

"But I'm not a fiddler, am I, Faith? You wanted it just as much as I did."

She nodded. Let him think he was right.

He parked up behind the mattress place—had he followed her when she'd been with other punters?—and cut the engine. She undid her seat belt. Slid her hand into her bag and curled her fingers around the short kitchen knife. Shifting so she partially faced him, she smiled to cover her disgust at his face cloaked by darkness, his eyes beady and glinting. She reached over and placed a hand on his thigh, rubbing, and leaned towards him, drawing the knife out, keeping it out of sight.

"I knew you wanted me," he said. "Bloody knew it."

She pressed her lips to his cheek—Oh God, oh God, I hate this—and brought the knife closer. Rammed the blade into the underside of his chin. He let out a cry of pain, and she yanked the knife out, switching hands so she could slice across his throat. She slammed her back into the passenger door to get away from the sheet of blood, him gurgling, her staring in fascination at the claret that looked black in the dark, the gaping slit in his neck. Wet soaked the cuff of her coat sleeve, and she got out of the car. Using her clean *sleeve, she wiped everything she'd touched, then walked away, the knife by her side.*

Someone would find him. The junkies were so far gone tonight, come the morning, they wouldn't remember she'd got into his fancy car. Halfway back to the lane, she cleaned the knife handle of prints and dropped it in a bin. Walked on, free of Tim at last. Just one more man to get away from, and her life could begin again. She folded her coat cuff to hide the blood, doing the same to the other side so they matched.

How calm she was. How at peace.

At the lane, she went with three other customers, in a daze. What she did with them, she didn't know, her mind elsewhere—in that car with Tim, reliving slicing his neck over and over again.

When she got home at two a.m., Reggie wasn't there, but a note was. He'd walked out on her, had moved his things to Kenise's, but that wasn't what pissed her off. He'd left Lemon alone, sleeping, not caring that their little boy might wake up and be frightened to find his parents weren't at home. She stared down at her son and vowed to be there for him no matter what, no matter who he became. She'd hug

him if he needed it, she'd encourage him to be whoever he wanted to be.

He was her life now.

The advert in the paper for women to give massages above a shop on The Benson Estate seemed like a gift from Heaven. Dad must be looking out for her. Faith applied, and her interview with someone called Vanda wasn't as daunting as she'd imagined. It became clear early on that massages weren't the order of the day.

"Sex," Vanda said. "That's what you'll be offering. Can you handle that?"

"I've been working one of the lanes on The Moon Estate for a while, so yes."

"What makes you think you can do this job—as in, switch from the streets to an upmarket establishment?"

"I like a challenge, and I want to be more than I am now. I want to be better. Plus, the money sounds good."

Vanda laughed. "Hmm, it's a damn sight more than you'd earn on the streets, I'll give you that." She cocked her head and studied Faith. "Our men will like you. Okay, I'll see if the boss is interested. Wait there a minute." She snapped a Polaroid of Faith then left the small office.

Faith glanced around. Ledgers lined a shelf above the desk, and a safe sat on the floor. A large clock on the left-hand wall ticked loudly to the beat of her frantic heart. If she got this job she'd be safer. She'd have a room and someone to oversee who her clients were. She'd earn a lot of money so could give Lemon a good life.

The door swung open, and Vanda poked her head round. "Mr Benson will see you now."

Faith got up, her legs shaking, and followed Vanda down the corridor. On the other side of reception, Faith averted her eyes from men sitting on sofas. Vanda went into another office and ushered her inside. Mr Benson, a big bear of a man with a full head of black hair, stood from behind his desk, appraising her. Faith felt like a side of beef.

"Take a seat," he said, voice gruff.

Faith smiled and did as he'd asked, her attention drawn to a little girl sitting on the floor playing with Barbies. She must be around seven, but what on earth was she doing here when punters sat out there, waiting for sex?

"Don't mind her," he said. "Her mother's coming to pick her up in a minute." He sat, leaning back, his *fingers laced over his stomach. "You'll be taking over from me one day, won't you, India?"*

The girl glanced up and smiled, then returned her attention to her dolls. Benson eyed Faith for too long. She wanted to get up and walk out, but she needed this job.

"I like what I see," he said.

Faith stared at him. "I won't let you down, I promise."

"You'd better not." He glowered at her. "Otherwise, there'll be trouble."

Faith swallowed. Her new life had just begun.

Chapter Thirty-One

Outside the roller door, George stared at Lincoln. Moon and Tick-Tock had not long arrived, and Lincoln strode towards them as if he'd been lurking for a while.

"He must have got my message," Greg muttered.

Lincoln reached them and raised a finger to his lips. Eight men in combat gear floated out of the darkness from the side of the access track. They jogged on near-silent feet, stopping behind Lincoln. Uneasy at the sight of their riot gear, polycarbonate plastic shields and helmets with visors, George took a deep breath. What did Lincoln know that he didn't?

"You're going to tell us we came unprepared," George said.

Lincoln scoffed. "You have no idea. The shit she gets up to. I've got a dossier on her. Photos, the lot. Inside man."

George nodded. "We saw him at hers and thought he was moonlighting."

Lincoln shook his head. "Nah, he's been watching Whitehall for a long time. I've been waiting to catch her doing something she shouldn't. He let me know tonight was the night. Something about her going against your agreement?"

"Hmm."

"My men will go in first—trust me, you'll be grateful for it. She'll have her blokes positioned all around where they've got your man, and they'll shoot on sight. With the shields, it limits casualties and we can shoot from behind and between my blokes. What kept you from going in?"

George bristled. "We were just about to when you showed up."

"Talking strategies, were you?"

"Yeah."

Lincoln inhaled sharply. "Right, a quick recce—and I mean quick, because there's not much time. When you enter, go through the doorway at the back. You'll see a corridor. Head down it. On the right is the door to the fridge."

"He's in a fucking *fridge*?" Moon butted in.

"Not just any old fridge. It's like a warehouse. Pigs and cows everywhere. Be careful, as her men hide behind the animals. Your friend is in the centre of the middle row."

Lincoln's army went ahead, stealthy, their military training apparent. Lincoln went next, then George and Greg. Moon and Tick-Tock followed, a gun in each hand. The overhead lights shone on Lincoln's bald head, his thick throat hidden by a black turtleneck jumper, his dark combat trousers and boots giving the impression he worked for the SAS. George wished he'd changed out of his suit into something more comfortable, another fuck-up on their part, but it was too late, and he'd tell himself off later.

In the corridor, he expected to see Whitehall's team, but it was empty.

"I can hear you!" she sing-songed, tacking a laugh on the end of it, the sound carrying out of the fridge. "We've been waiting for you."

"Fucking loon," Greg muttered and cocked his machine gun.

George did the same, his nuts tightening, anticipation doing a two-step through him. "Be careful in there, bruv."

"And you."

Lincoln's army stopped just before the door, stared at each other, then nodded. They sprang in front of the doorway, and a barrage of gunfire flared. The shields long enough to reach their ankles and cover their faces, stalling the bullets, the men surged inside. George took a deep breath then followed, wishing they'd put bulletproof vests on. The chaotic scene was too much to take in at once, animals swinging wildly, creating a macabre dance. He swept his gaze back and forth, assessing. Whitehall's men hid behind carcases, the ends of their guns poking out. Mrs Whitehall stood in the centre beside a hanging Austin, her gun pressed into the poor bastard's stomach.

Greg shot some bloke who toppled to the floor, and it snapped George into action. He went in further, past the line of shields, shooting his machine gun, peppering men and pigs and cows. Several of the Whitehall lot went down, including a big bastard whose features resembled a Neanderthal. George, hoping everyone covered his back, slunk down a row of pigs, the sway of the bodies making it difficult, the cold fuckers bumping into him, knocking him off balance. A bullet nicked his ear, and he clenched his teeth to stop himself screaming in pain, his eyes watering, fuzzing his view. Another volley of gunshots resonated.

An "Oh, fuck, no!" from Moon.

George turned.

Greg was down.

His *brother was fucking down*!

Pure rage and adrenaline stopped George from allowing fear to cripple him. He couldn't lose his twin. The other half of him.

Moon bent over and gripped Greg beneath the armpits, dragging him towards the door. Blood seeped into Greg's white shirt, matching the colour of his red tie, his eyes closed, his body limp. George's instinct was to go to him, to help save him, but Mad and Ruffian flooded his system, and he spun round, snatching pigs out of the way, heading straight for Whitehall.

"You fucking *cunt*," he screamed. "You bastard fucking *cunt*!"

He raised his gun and fired, shooting the shit out of her, Austin screeching at bullets entering him. George followed the bitch as she staggered back into a pig in the next row, firing, firing, her face flesh popping, spraying off her, spot after spot of blood wrecking her cream outfit with every bullet that penetrated her. She fell backwards onto the floor, and he dropped the gun, kicking her everywhere he could, anger and pain scouring his blood, the thought of walking through this life alone attacking his brain, taunting him, laughing at him. He was so *frightened*, of more than any bullet, more than dying himself. What would he do without Greg? What would he fucking *do*?

Memories flooded in, pushing him on.

"You mustn't say things like that, son."

"Why not? He's a fucking little bastard."

Greg wet himself laughing, his mouth open, chocolate stuck to his teeth.

God, George loved him. *Loved* him.

He got down on his knees, punching her, wrenching her hair, digging his fingers in and ripping her eyes out. He stuffed them in her mouth then thumped her nose until it caved in, thumped again until her teeth left the gums, until she didn't look like Whitehall anymore.

They sat at the table, side by side, Greg's thigh against George's. He always needed to touch George after Richard had gone off on one or when he was feeling weird inside.

George wasn't there for him to touch now, and guilt flogged him.

Still the anger surged, the fear, the thought of his brother, if he was alive, suffering pain — pain George had promised Greg would never feel. He'd promised to always protect him, but fuck, it had all gone wrong. He spotted a steel table to his right and launched over there, snatching up a large cleaver and going back to Whitehall. He put the weapon down and stripped her naked, wanting to see every cut he'd make, every spurt of blood, every bit of her intestines when he yanked them out of her.

"Mum'll be upset if you keep swearing, so pack it in," Greg said.

"She's not here to listen, so it doesn't matter."

Mad was taking over, and Greg had always known when to put a stop to George's insane side, but he wasn't here to do that now.

George picked up the cleaver, knelt, and brought the blade down. Over and over, hacking at her torso, slicing off her tits, carving her ruined face into four. He slashed at her arms, her legs, not stopping until her skin had been cut to ribbons. He dug his hands inside her stomach and yanked out whatever he could, wishing she was alive to feel the agony. The rage inside him boiled on, and he stood, kicking her over onto her front and attacking the rest of her. Stripes on her skin, blood oozing, her arse cheeks sliced off and left to fall to her sides. He parted her legs and rammed the length of the cleaver handle inside her, pushing and pushing as far as he could go. She deserved this, no matter how foul his last act was. She did. She *did*.

"I'll always be here to stop you going too far, you know that," Greg said.

Jesus fuck, but George was alone, no hand on his shoulder to prevent him from going to town.

No sharp words to get him to listen, to *think* about what he was doing. No tether, no buoy. Nothing.

He stood, stared down, and the mess she was in didn't assuage the agony roaring in his veins, didn't appease Ruffian who wanted to obliterate this woman, turn her into pulp and bones. Soaked with her blood, he pushed through the cows, the pigs, spotted Austin hanging limp, likely dead, and belted through the doorway. Lincoln's army filled the corridor. One of them pointed to a door along the way, and George barrelled down there, not wanting to see his brother dead but needing to anyway. To be with him. To hold his hand. To remember all the things they'd done together, glued to one another's sides, their telepathy, their bond, their every-fucking-thing.

Was he with Mum now? Was he?

George opened the door and stepped inside.

Greg lay on a steel table, eyes closed, face pale. Moon held his hand, and George would forever be thankful that this man had done that in his stead. Moon glanced over, his face dropping, his eyes red-rimmed. Tick-Tock turned away, swiping angrily at his wet cheeks.

Lincoln gave CPR, pumping Greg's chest and chanting, "Breathe, you bastard, breathe!"

It couldn't be over. Not like this.

"We're in this together, bruv, always," Greg said.

"I know. Just don't go dying on me, all right?"

Tears bulged, and an almighty wave of grief swept from George's feet to his head, engulfing him. He raised his blood-soaked face to the ceiling and screamed.

Chapter Thirty-Two

George, three hours later, showered and in a clean suit and tie, paced, needing something to do to occupy his scattered mind and jittery emotions. He'd cried so hard in that abattoir, sobs wrenching out of him, a never-ending stream of "Why?" choking out of his gaping mouth. They walked into danger every day, he accepted that, but Greg was never supposed to get shot. It was meant to be George, taking a bullet for his twin, adhering to his promise and always keeping him safe.

He'd failed, and it rankled more than anything he'd ever experienced. What would Greg want him to do now? Pace some more and torment himself? Dive headlong into a pit of depression? No, he'd tell him to get back to work, build their estate up, bigger and better, and fuck whoever stood in his way.

George checked his phone. Lisa had sent a message, and he stared at it, not giving a fuck that Bungle had got hold of Faith. That woman was the least of his worries now. She faded into insignificance, wasn't worthy of jack shit, but he supposed finding out what had happened to her would give him something to concentrate on.

When Greg had been taken away, Moon, Tick-Tock, and George had gone with him. Lincoln and his army had stayed behind to mince Whitehall and her men, then clean up—and deal with Austin, a casualty of war. His body would be taken to his house, and Janine would get a tip-off so she could inform Maxine. George couldn't bring himself to feel anything for *him* either, or his ex and kids. All that consumed his mind was his beloved brother. Lincoln had sent someone to Whitehall's to collect Austin's car and look for the drugs, and Lincoln's mum, of all people, had picked up Whitehall's dogs, saying she'd look after them.

"You're doing my fucking head in," Moon grumbled. "Either sit down or fuck off and do something. You're too antsy, still got too much anger inside you. Go and kill a few more people, for fuck's sake."

George didn't have it in him to bark a response. "There *is* something I could do. It shouldn't take long. Just got to check on Faith."

"What the fuck are you bothered about *her* for after what she's done?" Tick-Tock asked. "Jesus, whatever happened is her fault."

"Yeah, but unless you want me crying around you again, I need to do something."

"Go with him," Tick-Tock said to Moon. "Keep an eye on him. He's likely to go off his nut at the slightest provocation. He'll get caught in a rampage the mood he's in and he'll get arrested, leaving no one to run Cardigan."

Moon stood. Rotated his shoulders to get the kinks out. "Come on, then."

George walked out, feeling guilty for leaving his brother in this place that smelled sterile and whatever the fuck else hung in the air. There was absolutely nothing he could do but get his head back in the game as his twin would expect. He'd come back and sit with him later. Hold his hand.

In Moon's car—Lincoln was sorting their taxi—George stuck his seat belt on and stared out of the passenger-side window. The night seemed blacker than usual, or maybe he was seeing it that way, the stars few and far between. The scenery flew by, houses and shops, a park and a petrol station, all segueing into more of the same the farther they went.

On Cardigan, Moon said, "You're going to have to tell me where to go."

George leaned forward and programmed Faith's address into the satnav—he couldn't be arsed to say it out loud. Speaking seemed a monumental effort at the minute. A huge spark of light had gone out inside him, the shock of everything battering him, leaving a pathetic lump in his gut. He didn't know what to do without his brother by his side, it was weird not having him there to go and see to Faith. Yes, George went out alone as Ruffian, but that was different. Now, he had no one to call a knob, and Moon wasn't about to tell him he was a cockwomble and get annoyed at the amount of Pot Noodles he ate. The image of a jar of piccalilli popped into his head, Greg's latest fad, and an almighty lump broadened in George's throat.

"Fucking disgusting stuff, bruv," he muttered.

"What was that?" Moon asked.

"Nothing." George sat quietly for a while, then asked, "Got a lock pick on you?"

"Toolbox in the footwell."

George took it out. "Gloves?"

"Same place. Do you need bins or something? They're right there in front of you."

"No, I don't need bins. I wouldn't pick glasses anyway, I'd go for contacts, and my eyesight is fine, so piss off." He put the gloves on and threw a pair into Moon's lap.

The satnav, a bloke's voice, announced their destination was upcoming. Moon slotted his car three doors down from Faith's, and George got out. Automatically, he checked the street, glancing at all the windows.

He channelled his mind away from Greg and into work, walking towards Faith's door. Something caught his eye to his right, and he peered down at the kerb. A handbag sat in the road between two cars, and he stooped to pick it up. Moving to stand beneath a streetlamp, he dug his glove-covered hand inside and pulled out a purse. Flipped it open. A driver's license behind a plastic window. Faith's. He poked around some more. A passport and birth certificate. A cheap phone, which he switched off and pocketed. There might be incriminating evidence on it, like her telling someone Ruffian had given her a Cheshire, that George and Greg had sent him. The police could still get access to her phone account, though, but it didn't even worry him like it normally would. Another root around produced the usual shit. No keys, though, which was odd.

He hung the bag on his shoulder, imagining Greg laughing at him and saying he looked a right sort, and went to Faith's door. About now, Greg would warn him not to bust the door down and make a racket, and George would tell him to fuck off, to stop teaching him to suck eggs. His eyes stung, and he went to insert the pick but stopped. Someone had left the place unsecured. The door stood ajar. He slid the pick in his pocket and used one finger to push the door wider.

Moon came up beside him. "Oh."

"Hmm."

Light from the kitchen illuminated the scene. Scuffed blood and droplets marred the hallway floor. Faith's head sat at the end, staring at them, her matted hair clumped on top, wormlike tresses splayed on the laminate. Beyond that, her torso lay on the kitchen lino, a pool of blood beneath it, a film on top where it had been drying.

"If you're going in," Moon said, "you'll have to use the carrier bags in my car over your shoes as I don't carry any of that forensic gear round with me unless I know I'm going to get up to something. It gives Debbie the creeps when she loads the shopping into the boot, know what I mean?"

Moon sloped off to get them.

George took in the drips of blood on the stairs. Had Faith been attacked up there, sliced, then brought down here to be finished off?

Moon appeared and handed a couple of bags over. George got on with tying them over his shoes, Faith's handbag swinging round and clouting him on the knee, the strap creeping down his arm. How the fuck did women stand carrying these things?

"Didn't have you down for a handbag type of man," Moon muttered, tying off his second bag.

"Didn't take you for having odd footwear either. You've got one Tesco and one Aldi. At least mine are both Sainsbury's." He laughed.

And it felt wrong. He shouldn't be laughing, enjoying the banter, not when Greg—

"Doesn't feel right, does it, having a joke?" Moon said.

"No."

"What are you doing with a handbag anyway?"

"Found it in the road. It's Faith's."

"So she managed to get away but dropped it? She got chased and he took her back inside?"

"Dunno. Maybe he snatched her right off the street and she dropped it then. I don't even care. I'm only here because—well, it's what Greg would want. Come on. Let's go and have a butcher's." George stepped inside, hanging her bag on a hook beside the door. "We'll leave the kitchen until last. Saves us traipsing mess around, because I'm going to have to let Janine know about this."

"Why? Leave the front door open. A neighbour will find her, they can report it."

George shrugged. He usually cared about giving someone unnecessary grief, but tonight was different. Moon came in and closed the door to, and they stepped over the blood spots into a living room. The laminate went through into there, and blood spotted that, too. A wrist and hand lay on the arm of the sofa, positioned as if Faith sat and rested it there. Feet, cut at the ankles, the bones visible, stood on the floor in front, again posed where they would be if she occupied the seat.

Bungle had a sick sense of humour that matched George's.

Nothing else appeared touched, and no other body parts were in plain sight, so George walked out and poked his head into the little loo. An ear, in the sink, covered the plughole.

"Does that look bitten off to you?" He stepped back so Moon could see.

"Yeah."

George went upstairs, careful not to stand on the blood, his feet slipping on the cheap carpet, the carrier bags an accident waiting to happen. On the landing, he ducked his head into the bathroom. A hand, placed in the toilet water. A knee on the edge of the bath next to a bottle of shampoo.

"Jesus."

In what he assumed was her bedroom, her pelvic region lay on the middle of the bed, her severed thighs spread apart, the bloodied stumps going dark from the air getting to them. What appeared to be two elbows hung from the curtain pole at their crooks, and a length of her hair dangled from an earring display case, a piece of ribbon crudely tied in a bow at the top. He scanned the area, his gaze landing on a lemon-coloured teddy bear on the bedside cabinet. *Lemon for a Lemon*. It rested on its back, nipples over its eyes. Blood had soaked into the fur.

He turned his back on the room and entered another—Lemon's? Seemed so. The tops of both arms had been stuffed in with one of the pillows, the savaged ends poking out of the case. Her shins stood either side of computer speakers on a desk, books wedged between them. Bungle must have chopped her up and distributed everything, although why he'd do that was anyone's guess. For fun?

Moon said from behind him, "Reckon Whitehall told him to do this?"

"Fuck knows, but I've seen as much as I need to. I won't even bother going into the kitchen." There was still enough of the kind George inside him, it seemed, because he said, "I've changed my mind. I can't let a neighbour find her. What if it's a kiddie?"

"Fair point."

They left the house, closing the door, taking their carrier bags off. George turned them inside out, scrunching them into a ball, drawing one of his latex gloves over them to keep it compact. He stuffed that inside the other glove and took Moon's gloves to do the same. Greg would burn— No, Greg *wouldn't* burn them, just like hadn't burnt the gloves used when Benny had been murdered, they hadn't had time. Nor had they disposed of the guns.

George would have to do it.

He let out a long, shuddering breath and swallowed the lump in his throat. Got in Moon's car and waited for his friend to join him. The older man flumped into his seat and shut the door quietly.

"I hate this," George said.

"Hate what. This life? Your estate? All the crap?"

"Being with you. Not having Greg here."

"I know, son, I know." Moon drove away.

George put his seat belt on. He really ought to message Janine, but he'd do it later. The tiredness of grief overtook him. The responsibility of being him pushed down on his chest. He'd have to go and see Mum's best friend, tell her what had happened to Greg. He'd have to witness her shock, her tears, when all he wanted to do was hide away and cry. He'd have to stay strong for her, when he was the most broken of them all.

But not yet. Not yet.

Chapter Thirty-Three

Laura couldn't stop herself. She banged on Sneddon's door, eager to find out if Faith was there. She'd slept on it, waking up with an intense need to know what was going on. John was still in bed, the lazy bastard, and would be for hours. He'd stayed up playing games on his Xbox, selfishly shouting into his headset until four a.m.

She'd dropped the kids off at school, did a quick zip round Aldi, and now, here she was.

The door inched open, and Sneddon's watery grey eye peered out, half of his fleshy nose on display, riddled with thread veins. "What do you want?"

"Have you seen Faith?"

"What, that stupid cow from down the road? Snotty bitch if ever there was one."

"Yes, her. It's just she messaged me last night to say she was in your back garden. She was hiding from someone."

"Then she's a liar. She wasn't in my garden, and I'd know, I've got a security light that snaps on so I can catch what's-her-name's cats shitting on my grass. That light never went off all night."

"Are you sure it still works? I mean, the bulb hasn't blown or anything, has it?"

"I'll have you know I keep a regular check on it each evening by flapping my hand around. Yes, it bloody well works, and no, I haven't seen Faith." He went to close the door.

Laura put her hand out to stop it. "Did you hear anything? Like a scream or…?"

"I had the telly on loud, I'm going a bit deaf."

She lowered her hand and sighed. "Thanks anyway."

She walked towards Faith's, dread pooling in her stomach the closer she got. She rang the bell and waited. A few seconds passed, and she rang it again. She bent to push in the letterbox flap and peered through the slit.

She screamed, jumping backwards and staggering, landing on her arse. Heart thudding, she scrabbled for her phone in her pocket, dropping the bloody thing and making a hash of picking it back up. She dialled nine-nine-nine, the woman on the other end saying something, but the pounding of her heartbeat in her ears drowned her out.

"There's a head. There's a head in her hallway and… Oh God, there's blood everywhere…" She got to her knees, still not hearing the woman, and pushed herself to her feet, stumbling towards Steph, Faith's next-door neighbour, who'd come out to see what was going on. "Faith's head… She's dead. The police…"

Steph grabbed Laura's phone and spoke into it, Laura turning in a circle, a hand to her forehead, her mind racing. Had the twins done this, or was it that Bungle man? Would the police see Faith had contacted her and that she'd replied? She'd have to tell them but couldn't show the message because she'd deleted it. Would The Brothers think she'd dobbed them in and come after her? And if it wasn't them, would the police accuse them of Faith's murder anyway?

She sat on the kerb where she'd thrown the handbag last night. It wasn't there, but that wasn't surprising. Someone would have seen it on their way to work and picked it up, thinking they could nick the cards out of the purse. Oh God, what if the police found it and did tests on it? Her fingerprints would be picked up. She'd have to tell them she'd touched it. Not about the money, though, she'd never tell them that. It was safe in her knicker drawer, and that's where it would stay until all this had died down.

DI Janine Sheldon, her partner by her side, approached a woman the scene sergeant said had found the body—or had spied the head through the letterbox at any rate. This had the twins written all over it, or George specifically, and she'd brain them for not telling her they'd planned to bump Faith off. She plonked on a sympathetic smile to hide her anger and held her ID up.

"DI Janine Sheldon and DS Colin Broadly. Are you okay to have a word?"

The woman nodded.

"Laura, isn't it?"

"Yes."

The poor cow's red eyes told the story, as did her runny nose which she cuffed on her coat sleeve. Janine felt for her, it couldn't be nice to make such a discovery, so she held back the urge to tell her that things called tissues existed.

"Were you good friends with Faith?"

"Not really, but I was the one she came to if she needed help. Everyone else round here only tolerates her. She can be a bit rude."

Janine remembered her encounter with the woman when she'd called round to tell her about Lemon's death. "I see. You told the PC that Faith had messaged you but you'd deleted it. Can you recall what it said?"

Laura looked at the sky. "Um, something about someone called Bungle going after her and for me to get hold of The Brothers and—"

"Colin," Janine interrupted to stop Laura going any further in front of him, "would you mind asking the neighbour to make Laura a cuppa?"

Colin ambled off, probably glad he didn't have to be involved in any actual work.

"You were saying?" Janine prompted.

"She asked me to get hold of The Brothers for her and that she'd be hiding in Mr Sneddon's garden. I asked him earlier if she'd been there, and he said no."

"Did you manage to find The Brothers?"

"I went to The Angel last night, and Lisa sent them a message. I think Faith wanted them to rescue her or something? And I found her bag in the road, picked it up and saw her birth certificate inside. I got scared and put it back in case the twins got arsey that I'd touched it. Someone must have nicked it, because it wasn't there this morning."

"It's okay, it's in the house. Someone must have come by after you saw it. Can you remember what time that was?"

"The chippy shuts at half ten, and I got there just before that, so a bit after, on my way back."

"Okay. Did you see anyone acting suspiciously?"

"No, and I don't think I would have, because Faith sent that message a while before I left sewing club." She told Janine what time she'd arrived at the community centre and when she'd left. "So she was probably hurt while I was there."

"That gives us something to go on, thank you. Is someone at your house, someone who can sit with you? You've had a bit of a shock."

"My husband."

"Was he at home while you were at sewing club?"

"Yes, with the kids."

"Someone will be along to speak to him shortly. He may have heard something while you were out." Janine glanced over at officers doing door-to-door enquiries, then back at Laura. "Listen, if you're worried about getting into any trouble with the twins, I'll speak to them and let them know you're not involved in any way, okay?"

Laura's shoulders slumped with relief. "Thanks, I didn't know what to do. I didn't phone the police last night because the twins might have told me off."

"It's fine. Don't worry about it. Go home and…oh, Colin's back with your tea."

Laura took it, thanked him, and wandered past the neighbours who stood on the other side of the cordon sealing off the pavement a few yards either side near Faith's house. Janine still had the body to inspect, although she'd been warned by Jim, the pathologist, that it was in pieces, and she dreaded him telling her the cuts had been made with a circular saw.

"Colin, I need a minute to get myself together before we go in. I'm going to wait in the car on my own."

"Good, because that Steph woman told me to go back to hers and have a coffee and a biscuit. I think she fancies me."

She laughed and left him to it, changing out of her protectives. In the driver's seat, she checked she wasn't being watched and took her burner out, messaging the twins.

JANINE: AT FAITH'S. DID YOU KNOW SHE'S DEAD?

GG: YEP, AND IT WASN'T US.

JANINE: DO YOU KNOW WHO IT WAS?

GG: BUNGLE, WHITEHALL'S BLOKE, BUT HER AND A FEW OF HER MEN ARE DEAD, SO IT'LL BE A WASTE OF YOUR TIME GOING AFTER HER. BLAME IT ON THE

368

Network killing her, a stray who hasn't been rounded up yet.

That wasn't a bad idea, considering Faith's connection to Lemon.

Janine: Okay.

She deleted the messages and stared ahead. Cameron, her live-in bodyguard, stood with a crowd of other neighbours, keeping an eye on her. Not all of The Network employees had been caught yet—the refugee team knew their names, but the bastards and gone into hiding. Until they were all behind bars, Cameron was staying put. She was glad about that, as they'd been getting closer—close enough for him to kiss her quickly the other night, on the lips.

It was dangerous for her to fall for someone—dangerous because she wasn't relationship material—but she couldn't fight her attraction.

She sighed, got back out of the car, and put on fresh protectives.

Time to see what Faith Lemon looked like.

Chapter Thirty-Four

It was weird seeing George without Greg. Anna didn't know where the other twin was and didn't like to ask, especially because sadness filled George's eyes. While she didn't know him that well, the change in him was obvious. He was nothing like he'd been in the Noodle and Tiger when he'd given her this job. Back then he'd been confident, his usual swagger present, but now it was as if he'd deflated, his ego leaving the building. She wanted to ask if he was okay, but it wasn't her place, and besides, he might bite her head off, and that would be embarrassing in front of all the other stylists. He didn't seem the type to reveal his feelings anyway, and she had no right to pry.

The soft launch of the salon hadn't gone ahead, so the previously scheduled opening was today, two weeks later. Thank God the offer of free haircuts hadn't been advertised, because a long line of eager women waited outside, and it would be a lot more if they didn't have to pay for a new style. As it was, they were getting thirty percent off today, which explained why so many were out there. She spotted one of her old customers from the salon she'd worked at before having her son, Harper, and gave her a little wave. It was so good to be back in the swing of things. She hadn't realised how much she'd missed it. She didn't regret having Harper, despite who his father was, but her life hadn't been the same since. No more parties, no more getting drunk to blot out the past.

George stood by the till at the reception desk, staring into the street. It was clear his mind was elsewhere, his heart not in this, although he held her baby like he was precious. Harper slapped at his face, drawing George's attention to him.

"Little sod," George muttered. "Listen to me, son. You've got to be good today because Mummy has to go to work. Come on, we'll go and play." He walked past Anna. "If that's all right with you?"

"Yep, it'll save me worrying about him creating. If you wear him out, he'll probably fall asleep in about an hour."

George nodded and strode towards the back room, Harper waving at her over his shoulder. Anna waved back and blew him a kiss. That child was her life, her reason for living, and she'd never subject him to what she'd been through as a little girl. Vile thoughts intruded, clouding her mind, and her father's face loomed, his smile wide, his eyes gleaming. She shuddered and pushed the image away. Straightened her shoulders and smiled at the other stylists. *Her* stylists. George had given her carte blanche to run this place as she saw fit. She had so many plans, all written down in her new notebook, ones he'd given her the go-ahead for, one of them wine nights for women who worked during the day with no time to get a trim, sandwiches and cakes provided along with soft music so they could relax while getting their hair cut.

"Right," she said, "let's open up and get going. We'll make Under the Dryer a success if it kills me."

She unlocked the door, swinging it wide, and allowed the first few women to enter. In the flurry of taking coats and hanging them up, guiding people to their seats, Anna watched it all unfold, a glow of happiness in her chest. Life hadn't exactly been a bed of roses up until now — or maybe it had, except instead of lying on rose petals, she'd endured the evil prod of thorns. Still, George had changed all that, entrusting this business to her, and she was going to give it a bloody good go and make him proud. Maybe then that sadness in his eyes would go away.

She dived in. Spruced up ten customers, then her back let her know it was time to take a break. She stretched out the kink in her spine and moved towards the reception desk to sit on the stool there, a moment to catch her breath. Only three customers waited outside now, the staff had done a grand job whipping through all the others, and Anna smiled to herself. If every day was like today, she'd be raking in a lot of money.

About to nip in the back to make a cuppa for everyone, she paused at the sight of a man staring through the window at her, his face framed either side by posters taped to the glass. Her stomach muscles clenched, and she let out an involuntary cry, stifling it in case someone asked her what was wrong.

She'd thought she'd got away. Thought she'd never see him again.

She'd been wrong.

To be continued in *Rusty*,
The Cardigan Estate 23

Printed in Great Britain
by Amazon